Eth

Eth

Copyright ©2024 by M. Lalli Lassegard

Trade Paperback Edition

All rights reserved. No part of this book may be reproduced or transmitted in any form or by any electronic or mechanical means, including photocopying, recording or by any information storage and retrieval system, without the express written permission of the copyright holder, except where permitted by law. This novel is a work of fiction. Names, characters, places and incidents are either the product of the author's imagination, or, if real, used fictitiously.

ISBN-13: 978-1-965492-01-7

Edited by A.B. Hale
Book Design by A.B. Hale
Cover Design by Joshua Smyser & A.B. Hale

Published by
Blue Feathered Quill
Evans, Colorado, USA

Blue Feathered Quill | Trade Paperback Edition | August 2024

Eth | M. Lalli Lassegard — 1st ed.

License Notes

This book is licensed for your personal enjoyment only and may not be re-sold or given away to other people. If you would like to share this book with another person, please purchase an additional copy for each recipient. If you're reading this book and did not purchase it, or it was not purchased for your use only, then please purchase your own copy. Thank you for respecting the hard work of this author.

Eth

M. Lalli Lassegard

To Aria. This book is as much yours as it is mine. Thank you for trusting me.

Acknowledgments

Thanks for everything, Alex. I couldn't have asked for anyone better to share this writing journey with. Here's hoping for many more.

● Preface

Ð / ð   Eth /ɛð/   A letter used in both Old English and Old Norse. It is also used in Modern Icelandic and remains in use in names throughout the Nordic countries. It is pronounced as a voiced "th", as in the word "mother."

O Đ

I'd like to think that I've lived a fairly average life. There were a lot of highs, a lot of lows, and a lot of struggles in between. Though there are very few things I would have done differently, there are plenty of things that I regret. I'm sure you can relate. Should we start at the beginning?

From what I can recall, my earliest memories aren't very noteworthy. A hint of red tinsel. Snow on the windowpane. The color of my mother's eyes. The sound of my father's laugh. Certain warm smells. These are the faintest traces of recollection that I have stored in the scattered recesses of my mind. Sometimes in my endless daydreams, I think I can recall something else. Something more significant. I grasp at the tail of the thought, trying to follow it back to the origin, but it reveals itself to be just as fractured a figment as the other snippets. I sometimes wonder if any of these memories are even real at all.

What do I actually remember?

If I fall forward, move the scope of my mental spyglass to a more recent place in time, the insignificant shards become more distinguished. I can recall moments over the sensations. I used to play hide-and-seek with my father, giggling as I hid in plain sight behind the sofa. My mother used to brush my hair and I remember the soft feeling of her hands as she smoothed over the glossy mop that composed an unfortunate and childish haircut.

Still, these moments are as mundane as the earlier snippets. I'd like to find my first *real* memory. Something complete and direct, you know? I want to know what my first complete and coherent memory is. I might never know. No matter how long I spend staring out at the dusky sky, letting my eyes unfocus as my mind whirls in its fruitless searching, I might never know.

Never.

And is that such a bad thing? I don't think so.

Perhaps I would make better use of my time if I instead dwelt on more significant memories.

◉ Trolls and Elves

There was once a boy. He was small, quiet, and without many friends. He looked about as intimidating as a tulip; floaty and blond-headed, with freckles that betrayed an Irish heritage and eyes as light as the softest blue sky. His name was Niði and he didn't really do much outside of reading and daydreaming.

Every summer since he was born, his parents made a yearly trip to his grandmother's house south of Bergen, Norway. It might not be that surprising for me to say that he was never that thrilled to make this trip. I imagine that his feelings were always a little hurt at the prospect. The summer break between school semesters should be spent reading and studying, in his opinion, and being dragged to a strange old woman's home only to be shoved outside to 'play' really just interrupted his ideal plans.

"Niði!" His father strode into his room (actually, it was the guest room that had simply been reserved for him, but for the next eight weeks it would serve as *his* room) and with a bland but firm voice asked, "What are you doing in here?"

It wasn't a question that needed to be answered. In fact, it was one of those pesky questions that was really the old man's way of saying 'I don't like that you're inside reading rather than outside where every boy your age belongs'. And since this question was one that didn't need to be answered truthfully, Niði didn't. Instead, he pouted from the quilted duvet of the guest bed and stubbornly clutched the book he'd been reading.

His father didn't really care for this display of childish petulance. He didn't much care for how comfortable Niði was nor how invested he was in the *Nature Field Guide for Kids*. The day was sunny and beautiful. His son belonged outside.

"Come on, then. You're wasting the day locked up in here." For his benefit, he tried to appeal to his son's reason with a woeful sigh. Crossing his arms and leaning against the doorframe, he continued with a dreary line of questioning. "You should be outside getting fresh air and making friends, don't you think? Don't you want to go have fun? Don't you want to go make friends?"

The boy didn't respond. He was still sulking. Well, his father might have thought of it as such, but Niði knew that there wasn't a *correct* answer to this type of question, so he'd decided to not answer at all. This was, of course, in and of itself, an incorrect answer as well.

His father sighed again. "Put the book down and go play. You can come back for dinner, okay?"

This part of the conversation wasn't up for debate. None of it had been, really. Regardless, the young boy fixed his father with a crestfallen gaze before shuffling himself off the bed. In one last bold act of defiance, while he was turned from his father to collect his jacket off the floor, he tucked his book into his waistband and hastily pulled his sweater on top of it. Satisfied with his book-smuggling, Niði padded out of the room, past the tired stare of his father, and made his way out to the front door to put on his shoes.

The final bastion the boy had to pass to make it to the dreaded outside was his grandmother, a decrepit old lady who (in Niði's opinion) was probably a hundred years old or something. She was a pleasant enough woman, but a little scary at times, as the elderly so often are to children of young ages. As he skittered past her, she warbled out, "Don't get eaten by the trolls, love."

Niði shivered at the crone, rocking away in a blanketed chair. As much as he was nervous to do so, I'm proud to report that he remembered his manners. He turned, waved, and disappeared (finally) out the door with one last bob of his shaggy blond head.

For the first hour of his banishment, the boy wandered around the neighborhood, choosing directions at random whenever he encountered intersections in the sidewalks, with nothing but the sound of his shuffling feet for company. He found himself walking parallel to a forest and he eyed the little branching paths that fed into it from his main walkway with a scrunched and skeptical squint.

I understand what he felt. Surely, he was hoping to find the perfect place to hunker down and read without interruption from any adults.

He wanted to do what he'd already been doing, but without risk of discovery from his father, of course. Or any other adults that would tell his father that he'd been reading yet again. He just wanted to read in peace.

Slowing to a stop at another junction into the forest, Niði weighed his options. He looked left. He looked right. Upon confirming the utter lack of any other people around, he scurried into the cool shade of the looming trees. Not wanting to walk much further, he broke off the paved path, found a pleasant enough looking shrub tucked up against the curving arch of a tree, and settled himself in the inviting nook. Much like a cat as it spins around and stamps down the bedding before curling upon it, Niði too performed a small fidgeting ritual to get himself comfortable. Satisfied, he produced his field guide and went back to silently mouthing the words as he read contentedly.

At the same time, unbeknownst to Niði, another boy barely two years his senior faced a similar problem.

There was very little for this child to do indoors that wouldn't be disrupted by the screaming of a toddler or the shouting of a lover's quarrel. Viktor, a quiet boy, was tired of the constant din of it all. When he declared to his father that he was going to go into town to play at the park, his father had waved him off with a passive hand-waggle. Since the boy's younger brother was throwing a fit to rival the bitter jabs coming from his dad's pissed-off girlfriend, nobody had time for Viktor anyway.

Perhaps Viktor's father had seemed cold in this moment, but he knew his eldest son was responsible enough to take public transit alone and find his way around without issue, so why should he care if the joyless, silent boy left? One less person to worry about for the day.

And so, Viktor left with his father's blessing and little fussing. He hopped off the bus at the first stop inside the border of town.

I might've raised an eyebrow, had I seen a child withdraw a pocketknife from his pocket to slash at a nearby sapling. But, just as easily, I would have looked away once I'd seen it slip back into his pocket. Regardless, he retrieved his freshly cut walking stick and went about his way.

Most folks around town knew Viktor to be 'the quiet one' from an unruly family of immigrants. His father certainly hadn't earned any fans. His father's girlfriend had her own well-established reputation, one that I now know to be a fairly promiscuous one, but Viktor had no idea about that at the time. Whispers and smirks followed her like a veil, but the quiet boy never paid much mind to it. His brother, thankfully, at the time, was far too young to have judgments cast upon him.

There were only a handful of children Viktor's age that he'd come across. This was his first year in this town, having recently moved from his homeland of Iceland. Nobody had been enthusiastic to meet him. Likewise, though, knowing Viktor, he was also indifferent to their existences entirely. So this quiet and strange boy, having earned his own veil of whispers and hushed comments, roamed the parks and neighborhoods, forests and roads, all interweaving and connected throughout town completely unbothered and unapproached by anyone.

Left to his own devices, Viktor felt pleasant solitude more than anything else.

As he wandered into the forest, Viktor idly rubbed at a sore bruise. The sting of it faded from the sharp blows the day prior, leaving it as little more than a purple reminder of his father's ire. Not too concerned about the corporal punishment or the vague sense of neglect it left him with, he hummed his favorite song and tried to ignore the throb of his wrists under his sweater as he reached out and plucked handfuls of berries from the shrubs he passed by. He stashed them in his pockets for later and swished the freshly cut walking stick in front of him lazily.

It was around then that Niði could hear the distant sound of Viktor's approaching footsteps and the faint drone of his humming. He froze instinctively. Still as a deer he waited, thankful for the cover of the foliage of a willow bush to conceal him. The stranger didn't seem to be specifically approaching him, so the boy chanced a look between the branches, careful to avoid crunching any leaf litter as he did so.

There, coming steadily into view, was a dark-haired boy. The words of Niði's father echoed in his head, demanding he make friends here in his grandmother's town. Perhaps this would be his chance to follow his father's instruction. Perhaps. It was as good a chance as any, he supposed.

This new kid was by himself. He was maybe a little older. Taller, for sure. And he didn't look mean, at least not to Niði. Even if he did turn out to be mean, though, Niði was certain he could outrun him, so it probably wouldn't be a problem, anyway. As Niði weighed his options, the other kid made his approach, unaware of the shy boy as he struggled internally from the brush-cover.

Eventually, Niði gathered up all his bravery and pulled himself up from the ground. Dead leaves crunched loudly underfoot as he scrambled a little clumsily to his feet. The book was tucked under his arm securely and a few dried leaves clung stubbornly to the back of his sweater and ends of his hair. Emerging with a tentative step from his hiding place, he furrowed his brows in a look of grim determination.

"Hello…" Niði muttered nervously. As if he was hasty to rip off the social bandage, he charged on in a quiet voice, "Do you wanna be friends?"

Viktor, looking not-quite like a wild child, with his only-moderately tangled hair and just-slightly disheveled clothes, was very-mildly startled by the emergence of what he perceived to be an elf from the bush. However, his posture and expression remained vacant and bland (this permanent poker-face was something that he would become well known for) and he had no idea how to react or what to make of this sudden presence.

Later in life, Viktor told me that he'd wondered if it was a common occurrence for elven children to spring forth from shrubbery. His father was a stout believer in the Gods and their magic and had invested much time in raising Viktor under similar beliefs. Viktor even told me that he'd memorized many Eddic stories at that time in his life, but that he'd always remained a skeptic of the more absurd, mythical tales. In this moment, however, he kept the question of elven children to himself; he probably did ask his father about it later, though. Anyway, he stared back at this blond child. He stared for very nearly too long, to the point where poor Niði almost wanted to shrink back into the bush.

Niði felt fairly silly about the whole situation, actually.

Luckily, Viktor seemed to at least recognize the discomfort in the elf's shifting and he quickly shot his gaze away towards the trees above. And then to the ground. A pause. Then back to the elf.

Niði, crunching the dirt beneath his shoes, stared right back at Viktor with a curious squint. He had no idea if he was going to respond or not, but at least he hadn't said 'no', right?

Viktor struggled with the words in his head. This was something he'd had a difficult time with as a child, and something he still struggles with to this very day in both his native Icelandic and acquired Norwegian. Sometimes, he just needs more time to process something before giving a response. As it was, he hadn't lived in this town long enough for the words to reach his ears with ease, nor had he learned to emulate the sounds of the language perfectly enough himself to respond elegantly. So, he mulled the message over, trying to parse his desired response with a little frown.

Eventually (and mercifully for Niði), Viktor's inner computations ceased. He thought that perhaps it would be best to be polite to the elven child, if he *was* indeed an elf. Better safe than sorry. Outside of the large undertaking that could come of committing to friendship, he really didn't see a reason for why he shouldn't say 'yes' to the proposal, either.

Carefully, he nodded his head once. After another pause and another uncomfortable stare down shared between him and the other boy, he held out his hand. For a few seconds, Niði stared at Viktor's outstretched hand, lifted palm up and straight out in front of him. Was it meant to be a weird handshake? Or something else? It was impossible for Niði to know. This was surely the most awkward attempt at initiating friendship that had ever befallen the two quiet lads' lives. Regardless, he reached out and took the older kid's hand and, with a surprised chirp, he was pulled entirely free from the protective shield of the bush.

Side-by-side and hand-in-hand, the silence that followed the racket of the taller boy dragging the smaller boy from his hiding spot was surreal. Niði tightened his grip on his book, curling his arm up in front of his chest in order to hug the thing close to himself. Viktor's eyes flicked over him with what felt like an unasked question, but led to nothing, ultimately. Instead, he settled his gaze on their hands, feeling a nervous sort of buzz in his stomach.

Niði was too busy staring at Viktor's face to think of anything else to say. He probably should have asked to exchange names or something, but he was so caught up in the strangeness of the moment, that he didn't think to do so. A few seconds passed. Then more. More.

Surely, they were both thinking the same thing. What next?

Admittedly, Niði hadn't really expected his sudden request to be met with an affirmative answer and hadn't thought of a way to follow through. Viktor was seemingly perfectly content to stand silently and hold hands, but the smaller boy felt embarrassment wash over him as he stared bashfully at the ground waiting for *next* to happen. He didn't have to wait for long, though, because Viktor took it upon himself to start walking, leading his newly captured elf friend further into the forest, where they spent the day playing and snacking on whatever little fruits they could find growing in the brush.

And thus, the two met, strange as two children could be. Niði, a young 8-year-old, and Viktor, 10.

The next day, Niði wandered out of the house after very little goading from his father. In truth, he *wanted* to go play outside, if only to find his new friend again. And he did just that. The dark-haired boy was standing around one of the nearby entrances to the forest paths looking as aloof as he had yesterday. Without a word, he reached out in his peculiar way again (palm faced upward, arm outstretched between them), and the blond took his hand without hesitation. Viktor's hand was warm and a little sticky, because of the berries he'd plucked that morning.

They roamed the forest hand in hand, with nary a care in their minds. Just two kids enjoying a breezy day. When they stopped walking, they were in a small, grassy clearing. The space was no larger than a reasonably sized bedroom. A long-since-toppled-over log lay off to the side. Little wildflowers hugged the roots of the trees that encompassed the place. And the clearing was reasonably free of shrubbery. It looked like a good place to set up camp and relax. To Niði's young, imaginative eyes, it looked nearly magical—in essence, a secret garden, a quiet place to read and be left alone.

"Wow," he said, gaping a little in wonder. "This place is so cool!"

The taller boy didn't respond, but he let go of Niði's hand and flopped down in a particularly plush-looking plot of grass. Viktor hadn't spoken one word to him yesterday, so Niði wasn't sure if the boy spoke at all. He'd heard about people that were mute before. Probably read about it in some book. He thought it might be kinda cool to meet someone like that, much in the same way that children find any unique eccentricity to be appealing. But the mystery of Viktor's silence wasn't enough to hold Niði's attention.

The blond couldn't help himself and took to exploring the little enclosed area, flitting busily along the zone's edge. Withdrawing his favorite book from where it had been tucked under his arm, he paused to look at the flowers and touch lightly the leaves of nearby bushes. Every so often, he flipped open his book and stared intently between it and a plant before nodding to himself and moving on to the next eye-catcher.

Once he finished analyzing all that he could find in his book, he trotted over to where his new friend lounged himself and sat near him. He appeared to be dozing at first, but as soon as the rustling *whoosh* of

Niði's arrival hit his ears, he pushed himself up from the ground to sit cross-legged and faced him.

"Do you wanna see my book?" Niði asked the silent boy with a hopeful smile. Without waiting for an answer, he set the *Nature Field Guide for Kids* between them, facing Viktor. He opened it. As he flipped through the pages, he internally took catalogue of all the words too big for him to yet read and wondered if this older kid could read any of them. Most of the words were easy enough, but some of the scientific names still eluded him.

Much to Niði's relief, Viktor meticulously wiped his hands off on the front of his shirt, careful to make sure any sticky berry residue was completely gone before touching the book before him. With a ginger touch, Viktor turned the page and scanned the lovingly illustrated and photographed pictures of flora. One of his fingers settled on a bright picture of a plant he didn't recognize and he was reminded of the plucked berries in his pocket.

Withdrawing a little, keenly aware of Niði's curious gaze, Viktor hastily fished out the mildly smooshed remains of his plunder. A lot of the little berries had been squashed in his pocket, but enough of them remained intact to be identified. With his signature vacant stare, he held the berries outward towards his small friend.

Niði could hardly believe that his new friend was at all interested in his book. The only other person who ever cared to listen to Niði about what he'd been reading was his grandmother, so he was thrilled to bits that someone his age might enjoy the book too. He wondered if he could read with this kid and, of course, his little imaginative mind spun off in a billion different directions about what books he could bring next to show him.

But first, the berries.

He looked at Viktor, then the berries in his hand, then back at him. Then it clicked. "Oh! Do you want to see them in the book?" He didn't wait for a response. Nor did he expect one. The excited blond boy simply flapped the pages of the book in a happy flurry until he found what he was looking for. "Lingonberry, see?"

He pointed at the picture for Viktor to see and Viktor leaned over to look, hastily cramming the berries into his mouth as he did so.

"Vaccinium. I learned that word in school because I asked the teacher about my book and she read that word for me like that, so yeah, it's the scientific word for that kind of plant. Did you know that? It's kind of a cool word, though," Niði rambled.

His friend didn't seem to mind and, due to his silence, seemed to be a perfect listener. He watched attentively as Niði chattered, nodding here and there, occasionally looking down to the book to soak in what he could from both the blond boy's voice and the words on the page.

Once it seemed as though the smaller boy was done rambling, Viktor leaned back and looked him over. "Lingonberry…*Týtuber*…" he said in a small hush of a whisper.

Niði nearly jumped out of his skin. I'm not sure if he was excited or frightened, but hearing the sound of the other's voice for the first time had certainly shocked him. "You! Y-you can talk!"

A nod came back to him in response.

And then they stared at each other. The blond looked as if he'd seen his friend grow five extra arms, wonder and surprise evident on his face. The dark-haired boy had yet to wear any expression on his face at all, but Niði felt the distinct impression that he might have been a little surprised too.

"*Týtuber*…" Niði parroted after a few moments of agape wonderment. That was the word Viktor had said. It sort of sounded like Viktor had said a familiar word, but somehow it felt off to Niði. "Do you mean *tyttebær*?" The words were almost the same, and as far as the smaller boy knew, Viktor might have been trying to say that. Maybe he just had a weird accent?

"Maybe."

Not as shocked as before, but still surprised he'd gotten a response at all, Niði dumbly repeated this as well. "Maybe?"

Viktor looked at the sky. He looked at the ground. Looked to his left, back at the sky, then returned his gaze to Niði. With a deep breath, much deeper than his child-sized lungs could surely manage, he sighed heavily, then said, "*Týtuber* is the way I call it…It's the Icelandic word. I'm from there."

"You're from Iceland?! No way!" Niði was absolutely floored with excitement. It wasn't entirely uncommon to meet folks from the other Nordic countries, but he'd had yet to meet anyone from Iceland. "What's it like? Is it super different from Norway? Are all the words just different like that? Did you learn Norwegian in Iceland, too?"

Viktor sucked in a sharp breath and looked up at the sky. He looked to the left and released a sigh. "No. I only learned Norwegian…once I came to Norway." The hesitation on Viktor's end didn't come from any sense of nervousness or lack of confidence. It would be more apt to describe it as his voice trying to slowly eke out an answer that had been carefully considered.

"Wow!" Niði fidgeted with the corners of the pages of the book and very nearly bounced with excitement. "Say something else in Icelandic. Please?" He caught himself in time to remember his manners, thankfully.

Viktor looked up at the sky, looked down at the ground, up at the sky again, then back to his jittery friend. "*Jæja…Ég heiti Viktor. Og ég er frá Íslandi.*"

The smaller boy's face scrunched into a tiny frown as he listened, intent on figuring out if his new friend was messing with him or not. It sounded like he'd said something understandable in Norwegian. If Niði were to repeat what he thought Viktor had said, it would have sounded like '*Jai heter Viktor…O jai er fra Island.*' It was a little uncanny for Niði, honestly. To him, it sounded like Viktor'd just spoken with a strange accent more than anything.

He'd just realized that he'd forgotten to introduce himself or ask for the other kid's name. So, he responded hastily.

"My name is Niði. Yours is Viktor? Is that what you said?"

"Yes."

"I like your name." No response.

There were so many other questions now fighting for attention in his young mind, but he wasn't sure where to start, and it seemed as though Viktor wasn't too keen on handling too many questions at once. Niði couldn't quite describe it then, but Viktor doesn't like leaving questions unanswered, nor does he like having to answer them all at once. I'm not sure I can describe it any better than that, yet that's the impression the young blond got from the dark-haired Icelander.

Remembering to take great care in keeping his beloved book free of creases and damage, Niði shut it and slid it gently out of the way before poking around the grass in front of him.

Viktor had sprawled out on his side in the grass by this point and had stretched his arms above his head. Indelicately, he slapped around the ground, gripping tufts of grass and digging his fingernails into the dirt. And for a moment, it seemed as though the two boys didn't have much else to say to each other. This didn't bother Viktor, of course. I've always known him to prefer silent company to senseless chatter. He's always been of that preference.

But Niði still had a burning question that rose to the top of his mind above all others. "Can you teach me another Icelandic word?"

Under Niði's curious stare, Viktor looked up at the sky, looked at the trees, let his eyes wander until they settled back on the blond. He said, "*Vinur*. It means 'friend'."

⊙ Đ

I remember there being quite a stir in the small town where I was living when a man was murdered. I know this was something of a hot topic amongst the gossip-mongers and busy-bodies.

I get asked about it, from time to time. The whole scandal of it, that is. This was a relatively small town. Hardly any crime happened there. Naturally, this really was the most exciting thing that had happened in a long time.

To be honest, it was a bit too morbid for my tastes and I selfishly tried to avoid thinking about it. I *do* recall reading about it in the daily newspaper, and I remember that I only caught a glimpse of the story because I'd nearly spilled my coffee on a man on the bus out of shock when I saw it. I had to lean over to mop up my mess from the seat with a spare napkin I'd been saving in my pocket.

The whole town was changed after that, so they say. Folks say they were afraid to be out too late at night and all-around avoided the church near where the killing took place. They say there was an atmosphere of 'terror' and 'anxiety' afterward, but I actually felt a sense of relief. The town felt safer to me. Isn't that strange?

After a couple months or so passed, I'm pretty sure everyone forgot about it and moved on to newer, fresher gossip.

⬤ A King Needs a Crown

Viktor and Niði turned out to be quite the inseparable pair. After overcoming the awkwardness that was Viktor's persistent silence, Niði found that the older boy really *was* a nice person. He was never in a sullen silence, nor did he ever use his silence as a weapon against Niði's curiosity and mild chatter. I always found Viktor's tendencies to be endearing, really. If he didn't have anything to say, he wouldn't say anything. And sometimes it took him longer to respond than other people. He never filled the room with any unnecessary sound. It was just his way.

Rarely ever did he reveal his emotions, either.

At first, the younger boy found Viktor's blank expressions to be a bit taciturn and peculiar, but very quickly he became just as endeared to that aspect of him too. Just as with words, the dark-haired boy simply only ever emoted when it was important.

Unfortunately, Viktor would only further cement himself in the foreign-kid-with-a-bad-attitude-and-dishonest-parents camp with his numerous behavior quirks and odd habits, but Niði knew the truth. That truth being that Viktor didn't have a bad attitude, he was just a little blunt and bland.

They were both outcasts. In their own ways.

Niði was always viewed as the crybaby city-boy and was paid little attention outside of that. Though Viktor argued often that Niði was *not* a crybaby and, in fact, cried the proper amount for a reasonable person. This small kindness was one of the many reasons Niði became quite attached to him. Anyway, the younger boy was only ever around for two months at a time and he was too quiet to join the rowdy adventurous children and their games, so he often fell out of sight and out of mind to everyone else. He'd rather find somewhere quiet and out of the way to read. Have I ever mentioned just how much young Niði loved reading? I can't seem to stress that enough.

This 'outcast' label, however, was compounded for the both of them by the fact that they only ever seemed to enjoy each other's company.

From the first day they'd met to the last day of Niði's stay, they spent every day together. Viktor made it a habit to patrol the border of the forest, pacing around the pavement as he waited for his friend to show up. And he always *did* show up. Niði would scarf his breakfast and bolt out the door (before even his father could suggest that he go outside) and he'd practically sprint until he found Viktor.

They spent their days sharing Niði's books, taking turns reading, with the younger boy gently helping the older boy with his pronunciation. Really, Niði just preferred the sound of Viktor's voice over his own. He found this game of read-aloud to be the most effective way to get his friend to talk. And, admittedly, he rarely ever saw fit to correct Viktor's accent either, because there was some breathy, mysterious quality to it that the young boy thought was fun. Anyway, the point I'm trying to make is that this was the easiest way that young Niði found to get Viktor talking. Though even well into his adulthood, the quiet fellow never quite became fond of speaking.

This was also how the younger boy learned the most about his strange friend. If he could get him to read out loud, then he could more easily coax a follow-up conversation out of him. The most he ever learned about Viktor in one day happened because Niði had brought a book on Irish folktales to share with him.

The blond asked, "Does Iceland have any stories like this? Fairytales and stuff, you know?"

He waited a moment after asking. Though he'd only known him for three weeks, he knew by now that if Viktor was going to respond at all, he wouldn't immediately do so. But, this time, he did.

"Yes."

"Really? What are they about?" It was always difficult for Niði to hide his excitement whenever Viktor spoke.

Viktor, like Niði, wasn't one to raise his voice above a gentle mumble. It had a wispy quality to it and made Niði's native Norwegian sound somewhat whimsical. The younger boy, for whatever reason, was always entranced and clung to every word the older boy said. This time was no different, of course.

"...Do you know about Óðinn and *Freyja*, the gods?"

Niði bobbed his head in excited response. "Freyja is the one with the cat chariot, right?"

"Yes."

The young blond beamed across the grass to his dark-haired friend. Viktor stared back in his nearly vacant way, but Niði could tell by the slight tilt at the corners of his mouth that what he'd said earned a small piece of Viktor's approval. Bit by bit, Niði was learning how to read the subtleties of the other boy's expressions.

The conversation seemed to lag a little. Flopping over into the grass, Niði huffed a goofy laugh and pressed on. "So...the stories from Iceland are the same as the ones about Odin and Thor and Freyja and her cats and... Tyr and them, is that what you mean?" It just seemed to be that with Viktor, Niði always had to be direct in his questions, lest the conversation fade or the boy give unexpected answers.

"Oh," said Viktor, remembering the original question again. "Yeah."

"Wow, that's cool! I always liked those stories."

Viktor might have smiled. Niði thought he had, at least.

They fell into comfortable silence yet again, as so often they did when they spent time together. Though Niði would have preferred it if Viktor had spoken more, the young blond understood when his friend had said all that he would say. Viktor appreciated how understanding his new friend was about his brevity.

Silent, but not motionless, Viktor was twining plucked stems and flat blades of grass together into some sort of hoop. The younger boy had never seen anyone do anything like this before, and he was mesmerized. It was difficult to tell if Viktor was watching himself work or not, since the mess of his long hair had long since fluttered into his face and obscured half of it from any outside scrutiny, but to Niði, it looked a bit as if his friend was doing something wholly intricate and magical. He was simply entranced.

"What are you doing?" He couldn't resist asking.

Viktor didn't respond, but instead fixed him with a tilted-head stare that Niði would eventually learn implied 'wait and see'.

So, Niði did just that. He watched, hardly able to contain the fidgety excitement that so often overcomes the bodies of children. He kicked his feet down against the dirt beneath him, gripped at clumps of grass and poked little holes in the ground in front of him with already-dirty fingers. Viktor, far too stoic for any usual child, ignored his wiggly friend and calmly continued to work on the flower crown. It *was* a flower crown after all. It only took Niði a few moments to realize that. Or maybe 'guess' is a better word here. I don't think he realized so much as guessed. His folktale books sometimes had illustrations of maidens wearing rings of blossoms on their heads and that's what Viktor's project looked like, so that's what Niði assumed it was.

Eventually, once Viktor was satisfied with his handiwork, he got up on his knees and shuffled across the ground to unceremoniously plop it on the younger boy's head. Surprised, Niði pushed himself up on his elbows to look up at Viktor with a confused, "Huh?"

But the boy offered no explanation. Instead, Viktor turned and collapsed onto his back in the grass. He stared up at the leafy trees above him, those providing them cover in this out-of-the-way clearing he'd dragged Niði to for the day. Lazily, his hand slapped around the ground to the side of him, where he managed to grab a handful of grass and flowers to drop on his chest. He began weaving another knot of plants with his newly acquired materials.

After a few minutes of silence, Viktor took a deep breath. "I'm *Víkingur*," he said. Of his own accord, no less. Out of the blue. For seemingly no reason. Niði was almost too stunned to respond. Viktor had never, not once, not ever, been the first to speak between the two of them. For a silly moment, Niði felt afraid to respond. As if it would somehow return Viktor to his default silent state. But, luckily, his excitement won over his surprise and he *did* respond. "What, a viking? Do you have a boat? Like, do you fight monsters? Can I fight monsters with you?"

So many questions. Niði may have only had the life experience of an 8-year-old at the time, and he may have been skeptical of the existence of vikings in this current era, but something about the conviction in Viktor's voice made him keen to believe. As far as Niði was concerned, fairies and cartoon characters weren't real, but his friend being a ship-sailing viking was entirely within the realm of possibility.

With so many questions, Viktor retreated back into his mind to compute his answer. He rolled to his side and dropped the grassy knot, letting the scatterings of grass and flowers tumble down his shoulder. After taking his time to formulate a response, the boy finally addressed Niði's questions. "Yeah...*Víkingur*...It's my dad's boat. When the weather is good, I work on it with him. Monsters are too afraid to bother me…But, you're too small to fight monsters, so…you can't fight them with me."

The younger boy might have been stunned by the amount of words that Viktor blessed him with, were he not too busy daydreaming about seafaring and monster fighting. He had to agree with his friend, though, however blunt the assertion. With a little mournful nod, Niði conceded. "You're right. I have little arms and my dad says I cry a lot, so I don't think I can fight the monsters…"

His friend looked over at him, then looked back away to stare at the sky. He looked towards the trees, then looked back at Niði. He gave a small sniffle and smeared the back of his sleeve across his face, then said flatly, "You're the King."

So matter-of-fact and simple.

…But what did that mean? "Huh?"

"Every *víkingur* needs a leader to fight for. That's why I made you the crown. You're the King. I'm *víkingur*. I will fight all the monsters and bad stuff and protect you."

It was a simple explanation. A simple promise, and he'd said it as flatly and as confidently as he'd said anything. Niði laughed.

Viktor smiled for sure that time. Only a little. But he did.

And Niði kept laughing. He probably hadn't realized then how deadly serious Viktor's proclamation had been at the time, but he'd certainly been carried away by the whimsy of it having been said so sternly and casually. Just like that, he'd been elevated to a kingly status and had his own warrior to command. The crown of flowers for a small king and the rare curve of his friend's smile were all that stuck in his mind for the rest of the day.

Unfortunately, once Niði said goodbye to Viktor and returned home for dinner that evening, his father saw it fit to rain on his parade. He took the crown and tossed it in the garden. It *was* unfortunate, but such was his father's way. Flowers weren't very suitable for little boys and he wouldn't tolerate his son roaming around looking like a girl. That would have been simply devastating to his father's image, apparently. And so, away went the first of Niði's crowns with little ceremony and many silent tears.

Thankfully, Viktor would continue to make him many more floral diadems nearly every day they spent together in the little copse of wych elms, out of sight from the rest of the neighborhood. Viktor didn't care about what Niði's father said in regards to boys and flowers. He didn't even mind when Niði ran to him crying about the loss of his beloved first crown, either. All the other kids bullied Niði for being a crybaby—as did his father, naturally—but never Viktor. He simply, and silently of course, made him a new one.

I know that Niði mourned the loss of his first floral coronation very much, but he *did* manage to keep the second one. He has it to this day. Snuck it in under his shirt and carefully pressed it between the heavy pages of yet another one of his favorite books. For a large part of his life, this was his most prized possession. He liked to flip open the pages and touch the dried pressings whenever he felt sad. To him, it became a reminder of beautiful, soft things, his dear friend, and all the lovely days they spent together in their childhoods. And many other things.

O Đ

When I was a teen, I read a lot. It's always been a favorite hobby of mine, but I have a lot less time for it now than I used to. Or more so, I make less time for it. I have a lot of work that needs to be done, a lot of chores, a lot of social relationships to maintain. Well, maybe not a lot of relationships, but enough. So I find myself occupying my time a little differently now.

But when I was a teen, I read a lot.

If I wasn't stuck in class, I was holed up somewhere with a good book. And I was always drawn to non-fiction. I liked reading about history and science, animals and anthropology. I had as much of a love for learning as I did for reading. If I could learn while I was reading, that was simply the best.

I didn't have many friends as a teen. This was a little bit by choice and a little bit by circumstance. I preferred the company of a close few to a distant many, so to speak, and my anti-social reading habits certainly didn't foster an openness that would welcome any new friends.

I started to get more into poetry around then, too. There were a few authors that struck me for their fancy twisting of words and impressive prose. It was completely different from the realm of all the serious, not-fun non-fiction books I was accustomed to. So in a way, poetry became a nice break from my learning. Even now, I like to think I was still learning from poetry, whether I knew it then or not. I was learning the history of language usage and the creative way that minds conjure imagery for the intangible.

I never took to writing poetry myself, but as a teen, I dabbled here and there. I tried my hand at writing love poems, of all things. They were filled with all the feelings my 16-year-old heart could muster (and then some), and they were so meaningful to me then, that I almost feel embarrassed for myself when I reminisce on them. Looking back through those old notebooks now nearly makes me cringe and laugh out of my own skin, but I'm fond of those silly little things to this day, even so.

To think that the heart of a lovelorn writer was inside me at such a young age. I couldn't imagine where I would be today if my blossoming passion of poetry had become my future instead of where I find myself now.

But, sometimes, it's fun to imagine the 'what ifs'.

● Animal Bites and Daydreams

I may sound a bit predictable here, but…Niði and Viktor continued to be inseparable friends throughout the next few years. And I know I sound like a broken record, but Viktor's reputation didn't improve and little Niði continued to be too shy to make any other friends, so not much changed on that front, either. And why would Niði need to make any other friends, anyway? I suppose he had all he ever wanted in a friend crammed inside the complete package that was Viktor.

By the time Viktor was fourteen and Niði was twelve, not much had changed for either of them, except both of them were taller and a little more awkward with the dew of adolescence. I suppose, to pin down the more notable changes, Niði was much more freckle-dusted than before and Viktor had his hair cut to a more reasonable length just above his shoulders. But really, they still looked like a pair of gangly kids.

Something only Niði really noticed, though, was that Viktor was more talkative than he'd been a few years before. He still didn't talk much, and he used every word efficiently and bluntly, but he would initiate conversations more frequently than he had in their first year of friendship. They still were only able to spend time together over the short two months in the summer, which often led to the first week of their reunions being overrun with the chatter of the yearly recap of events. Obviously, Niði always had more to share than Viktor.

But, on one particular day, sitting together with his smaller friend on a park bench, kicking at the ground idly, Viktor remembered a question his teacher had asked the class a few days before the summer break began. He'd spent a lot of time dwelling on the question, acting much too serious for a boy his age (as usual), and now he wanted to throw the query onto Niði.

"What do you want to do when you grow up?" asked Viktor.

Niði's silver-blue eyes widened, blinked, then bore into Viktor's stormy grey ones. "Oh…Hm. I dunno. What about you?"

Fair enough. Viktor had had weeks to think about the question. He didn't expect Niði to have an immediate answer. After nearly ten seconds, he said, "I don't know what I *want* to be. But I think I'll *have* to be a fisherman."

It was a very Viktor-like response. His father owned a boat after all, and that's what his father did. Viktor had been commissioned into helping season after season and he may as well have been his father's apprentice at that point. He probably only ever envisioned himself as taking on the torch, whenever his father was done with the career.

But the blond boy didn't like the answer. Not really. And his brow furrowed a little to show his disapproval.

When Viktor didn't react to his frown, Niði said, "You shouldn't do something just because you *have* to. You should grow up and do what you *want* to do."

"Okay."

"Well, you like to read and you like the *Eddas* and stuff, right? Maybe you could be a writer instead. Or you could be someone that does stuff in a museum. Or like…a historian."

No response.

While he waited, just in case Viktor might want to respond, Niði kicked a few pebbles from under his shoe into the middle of the sidewalk. When no response came even still, he continued.

"I might become a writer, or maybe I'll be a drawer or something… Oh! But, actually, I think it might be fun to be a botanist."

"What's that?"

Niði giggled at this. It wasn't often that he knew something Viktor didn't, and he was always delighted to be able to teach his friend something new for once. I'm sure you can relate to this feeling very well. Sharing knowledge with your peers is always such a fulfilling way to pass time.

Just as he was about to unload upon his older friend the wonders of botanical science, he caught sight of approaching figures on the sidewalk and froze. Viktor, to his credit, noticed the shift in Niði's posture and turned his head to look in the same direction.

A handful of teens, rowdy things, ambled ever closer, joking loudly with each other. Their voices were just now reaching Viktor's hearing threshold, but he couldn't quite make out their faces yet. Still, he understood implicitly Niði's deer-in-headlights reaction.

He grabbed the blond's hand and started to get up. He was fully ready to leave and lead his friend away from the trouble before it arrived.

But this action shook Niði back into the present and, with his return, a little petulance gripped him. In the smallest hint of a whisper, and with a dash of sulk, Niði said, "I don't want to have to run away and hide every time they come around."

Now it was Viktor's time to freeze in place. He could hear in Niði's jaw-clenched hiss that he might be a moment from shedding tears, but he wasn't quite sure what to do about it. Viktor was stuck physically somewhere between rising from the bench and comfortably sitting, but he remained poised while he weighed both the nuisance of the approaching loud-mouths and his sympathy for his small, too-frail friend. The options danced around his mind for a moment before he settled on his decision.

Whatever Niði wanted to do, Viktor would do.

He sat back down, but still held onto his friend's hand.

Now, I know for a fact that nobody likes loud, obnoxious teens. It's just the way of the land. Every land. Even loud, obnoxious teens don't like other loud, obnoxious teens. And everyone thinks of themselves, at that age, as if they themselves are not loud, obnoxious teens. Niði, despite how he acted around Viktor, was not a loud, obnoxious teen himself, but he was often a target of their insults.

Regardless, Viktor sat tensed and coiled, ready to spring at any moment, dreading the approach of these loud, obnoxious teens. He was staring straight ahead, hoping to somehow remain invisible to this group of nuisances, but I'm sure even he knew how fruitless this hope was. Niði was doing more or less the same, but he was prepared to bolt whereas Viktor was very likely prepared to throw a punch. They must have looked like a pair of idiots to the fast-approaching group, because their bone-headed banter made the transition from internal friend-teasing to external Viktor-Niði-bullying.

"Fuuuuck! I thought the baby didn't come back this summer, hadn't seen it around lately!" Goon number one teased.

This amused Goon two greatly and they shared an ugly, sardonic laugh together.

Goon three found it fit to chime in with, "Think he's gonna cry like a little bitch again? Gonna cry to his mommy about us?"

Viktor almost stood up, but something about the tiny jerk of Niði's head shake and the squeeze of his small hand against his own kept him fixed in place. The poor awkward lad was trying his best to stare forward and ignore their jabs and at the same time keep his very protective friend from starting a scuffle in the middle of the park. What upset the blond the most, and certainly didn't help his case were indeed the tears burning just at the edges of his eyes. "Look!" Goon two squawked. "Actin' like a pair of fags, holding hands in the park. Is the little baby on a date?! Must think he's all grown up now!"

A particularly shrill girl in the role of Goon four squealed a horrendous laugh, and the tears overflowed from Niði's struggling eyes.

"Fucking loser baby fa–"

Niði squeezed his eyes shut before the end of Goon two's insult, bracing himself because he knew what was going to be said next. Everything happened too quickly then for Niði to know the exact exchange of events, though he knew he felt Viktor's hand rip from his at some point. He felt the surreal absence of warmth at his side, the void where their hands were once clasped, and heard the choked gasp of the cut off insult. He didn't dare open his eyes.

Niði didn't see what happened next. He still doesn't fully know to this day what exactly transpired. He'd kept his eyes tightly shut and tried to stifle his shaky, pathetic little sobs with his chin tucked firmly down against his chest and waited for it to be over.

I couldn't possibly fully explain the noises that he heard while Viktor lost his temper on the little group of four goonling teens, but there was a lot of grumbling, shrill screaming from the girl as well as her exclamations and obnoxious laughter while she shouted, "Oh my god! Oh my god! He's like a rabid dog! A rabid pet dog! Gross! Fucking fags!" and whatever other insults passed through the void in her head. There was the distinct rustling of fabric, the gritty scratch of shoes on pavement, a few thumps and reactionary yelps, and not much else.

I just know that once Niði dared open his eyes again, the problem had been dealt with and the loud, obnoxious teens were walking *wherever* they were going for the day. But the first thing he noticed was Viktor. He *really* noticed Viktor.

His expression was as bland and unchanged as always, but somehow, Niði felt as though he was looking at his friend for the first time. Maybe not for the first time ever, but for the first time in a very long while. The teens were easily at least Viktor's age or older, but he was taller than them—he was a tall kid. And though he looked a little freshly battered, his disheveled clothes revealed older bruises on his wrists and little cuts that lined his fingers. Why hadn't Niði at least noticed the cuts before? Viktor had a nosebleed, a few fresh welts, and a brand-new tear in the collar of his shirt, but aside from some wild tangles in his hair, he didn't look much worse for wear.

Viktor didn't seem to notice the extent of his own injuries, though. Well, he was too busy staring at the backs of the rambunctious group to notice much at the moment. I always wondered what could have been going through his mind then. Did he hit the girl at all? Did they gang up on him? Did he leave any of them as battered as they left him? In the end, I suppose it didn't really matter.

Anyway, he came back to the bench and sat back down after a few more moments of staring. He rubbed the back of his sleeve under his nose once, but aside from that gave no reaction to the steady little stream of blood leaking out of his face. In a mixture of concern and awe, Niði gaped at him. This was the first time Viktor had ever gotten into a fight for him, and never had he looked cooler.

"Are you okay?" Niði asked, swallowing down the shivering remnants of his sobs.

Viktor gave him a sideways glance. "Are *you* okay?"

He really wasn't. But the absurdity of his best friend, covered in bruises, old and new, *still bleeding*, asking *him* if he was okay, stirred a laugh out of him. He just couldn't help himself, and for a good, long moment, Niði couldn't stop laughing. He was so caught up in the moment that his laughter chased away the last of his tears.

Even stoic, quiet, strange, bleeding, bruised Viktor managed a small chuckle, though, it looked a little strange coming from his expressionless face. He quirked one corner of his mouth up at Niði, who took it as a smile. Niði smiled back.

"…But are you okay, really, Viktor?"

"Yeah. Are you okay, really, Niði?" Viktor gently mocked back, still wrestling with a smirk. This was some new side to him that the small blond hadn't seen before. Had Viktor always had this cheeky sense of humor? Niði wondered where it had been hiding this whole time and why it chose to reveal itself *now*.

"Yeah, I'm okay. Th-thanks, Viktor…"

"Good. Fuck them. They're stupid."

The bluntness startled another laugh out of Niði. When had Viktor started swearing?

But his happiness was short lived this time. Another thought gripped him suddenly in the wake of the encounter and he just couldn't shake the ensuing insecurities that remained of it. "Do…you think I'm a baby?"

The smirk faded from Viktor's face and was replaced with his standard blank stare. He stared for a while. A seemingly infinitely long while. Niði had to look away nervously, cracking under the pressure of Viktor's unreadable expression. The poor, sensitive blond couldn't handle the weight of Viktor's silence after asking such a sensitive question.

The tall boy looked away to the sky, towards the ground, and back to Niði. He finally said, "I think that you cry a lot, but I don't think that's a bad thing. It's just how you are."

It wasn't the answer Niði was looking for, if he was even looking for a specific answer at all. He wasn't sure if he was hurt at all by it, and he was prepared to defend himself against the accusation, but Viktor surprised him with more elaboration.

"I like how you are, though, okay? I just like you. I don't care if you cry." Niði almost started crying again, but from some mixture of relief and gratefulness. Maybe even happiness. A little frustration, perhaps, for the simplicity of Viktor's answer. There was no flattery to it, nor was there any criticism. It was a string of simple statements that came so easily from the dark-haired boy and yet they meant everything to Niði. But he felt a distinct twinge of regret for the question he didn't quite have the courage yet to ask. I don't think he even knew yet what he wanted to ask.

Regardless, it was a complex emotion for a 12-year-old to have to explain. Whatever the reason for his wave of near-crying, though, he knew for certain that he was at least happy to hear that his friend liked him. Even if he tended to cry a bunch.

● Đ

I met a friend for lunch once after graduating from university. It was a very brief meeting and we had a very short conversation. It was a fairly upsetting one to have, and I regret reconnecting with the person greatly. I suppose it gave me closure in many, many ways, yet had I predicted how the discussion would go, I don't think I would have gone.

On the walk home, I saw a group of people out in an empty car lot. They were dressed as if they worked in an office, business casual, and had come out to the lot while on lunch. I watched them as I passed by and was warmed to see them throwing a tennis ball against a nearby wall, taking turns catching it. They were all smiling. I found myself smiling, too, even long after they'd passed from my sight.

I don't recall the weather that day being particularly warm, so I'm not sure what possessed them to go outside and play together, but it reminded me of my childhood a little. It reminded me that sometimes, everyone deserves a break to run outside and just have a little fun. I wish everyone treasured moments like those a little more. We all deserve a little play here and there.

● There is Always Forever

Since, for a large part of his childhood, Niði only visited during the summer between school sessions, the weather often was decent enough for both him and Viktor to play outside and be left to their devices. Sometimes, it rained. Sometimes, it was windier than usual. But for the most part, the weather was reasonable enough for them to tough it out outside.

Niði didn't know it at the time, but Viktor would stand around their agreed-upon meeting place, which was just a specific junction in the sidewalk that turned off into forest they frequently played in, every day. This included bad weather days. On those, though still very, very rarely, Niði was kept indoors by the fussing of his grandmother. So there were at least a handful of days where the two boys weren't attached at the hip. Only a handful. And it made them both a little miffed for the circumstances of being kept apart from each other. I agree with their contempt, though. Who wants to lose a precious day of running around with their best friend?

On one particular day, a good weather day, Viktor was waiting as he always did at the little junction. Very rarely was Niði the first person there, though he always tried to scamper out of the house as early as possible. Who knew how early Viktor got there or how long he stood there for?

The blond, freckled boy trotted up to his friend excitedly, having decided to run to him as soon as he rounded the corner and saw him.

"Hi, Viktor!"

Viktor didn't respond, but held out his hand and waited for Niði to take it. This was their usual ritual. Though Viktor was much more talkative than he had been, he still rarely spoke at all until the two of them were well tucked away in one of their favorite hangouts. As for the handholding, this was just something Viktor had always done, ever since the first time he'd met Niði. He'd take his friend's hand and guide him away to wherever he had in mind for where they should be for the day.

As they walked the little paved path and passed by willows and shrubs with little berries, he thought a little bit about Viktor and their friendship. They'd been friends for a few years now. What did he know about Viktor at that point?

Viktor was two years older than him, had a birthday in the middle of autumn, and had a brother that was years younger than Niði. Viktor didn't really like to talk about his family, so he could be wrong about that. He hadn't claimed such recently, but he was still a viking in Niði's eyes. He just sort of had that energy to him. Strong, brave, stoic, dependable. That was how Niði saw Viktor, and that's how he saw vikings too. Viktor was tall and muscular, didn't like to brush his hair, and pretty exclusively wore red or black clothes.

Those were all shallow things, though. What else did Niði know? Viktor was quiet, though not just in the way that meant he didn't talk a lot. He was a quiet talker, and his voice was always soft and airy, almost like he had to hiss some of the letters to get them out. His voice floated more than it projected, when he spoke at all. Just because he didn't speak, though, didn't mean he was unhappy or annoyed. He would rather listen to Niði speak instead, which was a little silly because Niði felt the same way about listening to Viktor speak.

What else?

He was gentle and kind, at least compared to a lot of the other rowdy boys around town. A lot of them only cared about being better than each other at sports, new music on the radio, and throwing rocks at lakes. They did 'boy' stuff. As the blond's father was prone to say, "boys will be boys".

But Viktor didn't do those things. At least, Niði never saw him do any of those things. He never really seemed to act like the other boys did. Thinking about it, Niði had never seen Viktor with any other friends, either. Even though Viktor was a little expressionless and quiet, he still seemed like he belonged more with the other boys than he did with Niði.

Niði definitely thought that Viktor was better at being tough and strong than he was. He saw Viktor get into a few fights and saw him climb trees and saw him do this and that and all kinds of things. He saw his friend do everything that his own father would probably like if Niði did more of. But he also saw Viktor do all kinds of things that he'd assumed only girls were allowed to do. Would you believe me if I told you that it was Niði's father that drew all these lines in his mind? Well, Viktor had a distinct habit of blurring those lines.

Viktor made flower crowns and told Niði it was okay to cry. He held hands and (well, Niði had never seen this happen, but Viktor himself said he did this) he took care of his brother and did his own cooking at home. Viktor was, by all means, a kid with normal, healthy interests, in my opinion. But to Niði, at that age, he was a bit of an odd person. A bit of an enigma. Even though they were a similar age, Viktor always seemed a little bit wiser to the world than Niði—in a strange way, a little bit like a parent. Maybe not. Maybe more like an older brother. But not quite that, either. I'd describe Viktor as having caregiving qualities, which were confused by the household paradigm that Niði was used to. The timid blond's home was ruled by distinct lines and borders; his mother was the caregiver and his father was the law of the house.

From what little Niði had overheard in passing from his own parents and from the other kids, Viktor's dad was a foul-tempered alcoholic. But he wasn't quite sure what exactly that meant as far as how Viktor's home life looked. The blond hadn't heard anything about Viktor's father's girlfriend in a long time, so he wasn't sure if she was still around or not, but it wasn't the sort of thing he felt comfortable asking about, either.

Honestly, Niði knew Viktor better than he thought he did, and Viktor knew Niði likewise. They were both fairly observant, as far as children go, especially when it came to each other. So, what did Viktor know?

He knew that small Niði struggled to make friends due to his shyness and nerves. He knew that Niði loved learning, reading, and looking at nature. There was a period of time where Viktor *tried* to figure out exactly how many freckles were on Niði's cheeks, but could never finish counting them before Niði moved or they got distracted by something else. So Viktor didn't know that. But he did know that Niði's favorite color was purple.

Of course, Viktor also knew that his friend was a little sensitive and a little weak physically, too. He knew that he liked Niði and appreciated how curious he was. Niði was patient and friendly, reminded him of an elf, and if you got him talking, had quite a lot to say about the world. Niði didn't have any siblings, and though Viktor never really asked about his parents or anything, he knew that Niði sometimes struggled to see eye to eye with his father. The two boys had that in common. And this commonality is largely the reason that neither of the friends would go to each other's houses.

Viktor didn't want to expose Niði to the sheer chaos that was his family. Aleksi, his brother, was young and loud and a rampant menace. His father was indeed struggling with alcoholism and temperamental control, and the on-and-off girlfriend was a tornado of absurdities whenever she was around. Viktor could hardly stand the noise and violence of it all, and if he could help it, he would keep Niði from ever having to endure it, too.

Likewise, something about the idea of Viktor meeting his father filled Niði with an indistinct dread. There was no proper explanation for this gut feeling, but in a way, I understand it to be a bit of comparative-anxiety. What I mean by that is Viktor was, in Niði's opinion, a much better model for what a *real man* should be like. If Viktor came and spent time at his house and met his father, then of course his father would say things like, "why don't you act more like your friend? Why don't you try to be better? Stronger? Less of a crybaby?" Not that he would have held it against Viktor at all, but he didn't want to give his father another reason to deflate his already shaky self-esteem.

So the two mutually came to the same unspoken agreement, each for their own reasons. Both of their homes were off-limits.

They had plenty of hiding places around town to play make-believe vikings and read books together, anyway. Which reminds me, Niði really liked listening to Viktor read out loud. I mentioned this before, but it's worth saying again. Everything always sounded better to Niði when Viktor spoke. Anyway...

"Huh!" The blond little daydreamer collided unceremoniously with Viktor's sturdy shoulder as he halted at their destination. "Ah! Sorry!"

His dark-haired friend turned and looked down at him with a tilted head. One corner of his mouth lifted in the hint of a smile. Niði looked away quickly, a little embarrassed, and took in his surroundings. They were in a clearing. Well, not just any clearing. They were in the first clearing Viktor had ever brought them to. It was Viktor's favorite spot to go, but they hadn't been there in a week, so in a way it felt a little like returning home.

There was the log, collapsed and horizontal, old and smoothed with time, that Niði liked to sit on the ground and lean back against. The creeping wildflowers that clung to the sides of roots and tree trunks were as bright and friendly as ever. Everything still felt a little magical and distinct from reality in a way that made Niði *want* to believe in elves and monster-fighting vikings.

It was a place that was a little off the path, out of the way from literally anyone else. Reality didn't have to exist here if Niði didn't want it to, and that's what made this place so special to both of them. Nobody had ever found them there before, so there was no reason to worry about any of the other kids making drive-by insults at them, and it just felt safe.

Regardless, now that they were where they needed to be, Viktor let go of Niði's hand and wandered around in search of a good stick. Niði's mind wandered in tandem with Viktor's steps, and he found himself settled on the ground against the log before he knew it.

"Hey, Viktor?"

No response but a quick flick of his eyes towards his friend. Niði knew this as the 'go ahead' glance.

"Do you think we'll be friends forever, like until we get old and stuff? Until we die?"

Now the older boy's attention was caught, and he ambled over to the smaller boy, giving up temporarily on his hunt for the perfect dirt-doodling stick. He sat down on the log next to Niði, then said, "Is that possible?"

Niði started to weave his hands through the cool grass and smiled a little at the question. "Of course it's possible. Lots of people stay friends for years and years. Like, my mom is still best friends with her friend that she met in school from when she was like six, you know?" He rambled a little, frantically palmed the grass beneath him and looked up to stare at Viktor. With a nervous little stutter, he asked him, "We could do that too, right?"

No response. Niði hazarded a glance away from him and when he felt brave enough to return his gaze on Viktor, he saw that his quiet friend appeared to be in deep thought. So the small boy waited until his friend was ready to talk. Much to his relief, Viktor's response was just as he'd hoped.

"Yeah. Okay, let's do that, then."

O Đ

Let's put it this way instead, what do you remember about your life? I know that I started this trip down memory lane just because I wanted to find my earliest memory, but what is there to remember? There were a lot of distinct moments that I felt were so significant that I might cherish the memories of them forever. Distill them into the perfect snapshot, if possible.

I can recall so much, given enough time. But am I remembering the right things? Is what I remember really what happened?

What if I'm accidentally making things up or misremembering? And do you think I'm leaving out anything important?

When I remember things, I sometimes skip around a little, but I think we all do that. Especially when it comes to childhood, you know? It gets a little fuzzy way back there and I can hardly remember if something happened when I was ten or eleven. I'm not sure it even really matters.

I think what matters most is that you don't think I'm leaving anything important out.

What else do you want to know about Viktor and Niði from when they were kids? There's not much to say, really. Do you wonder what they did when they were apart from each other? Fair enough. I'll try to fill in some of those gaps, then. But briefly, because I *really* don't think it matters that much in the grand scheme of things.

Okay, I'll start with Viktor. But, I have to admit that he didn't tell me any of this until much later in life and there are some things I still probably don't know about him. I'd like to think that I definitely know more about him than anyone else, though.

So, Viktor. Let's talk about him for a minute. We'll talk about Niði after.

◯ Viktor

Viktor Sorensson was born in a small town in Iceland called Húsavík, where his father worked as a boatsman or fisherman of some kind. The boy was an infant at the time and he didn't have the best of relationships with his father until much, much later in life, so he's not even sure what his father's job was. His father had an on-again-off-again girlfriend from Norway, and once she'd gotten pregnant, Viktor's life became much louder.

For a few years, his family remained in Iceland until his father's girlfriend had decided she'd had enough of the island. They moved to Norway after Aleksi's third birthday when Viktor was nine, nearly ten.

As often is the case with younger siblings, his baby brother Aleksi was loud and needy. His father, not the sort of man to be very patient, whittled away his days either drinking or working on his boat. Viktor was expected to help most days, leaving his father's girlfriend home alone with Aleksi.

For the most part, Viktor did well in his classes, both before and after moving to Norway. He overcame the language barrier quickly with supplemental tutoring sessions, though it wasn't as if the transition from Icelandic to its sister language Norwegian proved to be as challenging as, say, Icelandic to an unrelated language like Cantonese might be. He then met Niði, immediately after his first school term in Norway.

Once summer ended, Viktor went back to his classes and spent a lot of his days at home. His father was a fan of using corporal punishment for the slightest transgressions, so to avoid any unwanted questions from any outsiders, Viktor made sure to wear long-sleeves and long pants whenever possible. Jeans and hoodies were his most iconic attire.

The upside, in his father's girlfriend's opinion at least, was that when it wasn't summertime, Viktor stayed home more frequently and helped deal with young Aleksi. He still spent a good amount of time helping his father on the boat. Ultimately, once Viktor hit 16, his father's girlfriend left them all. She'd had enough. In Viktor's own words, "she was a terrible mother and a terrible partner, but despite that she finally learned that she didn't deserve to be treated the way my father treated her."

What else is there to say about his childhood?

Well, I can say that a year before, when he was 15, he made a new friend in an artsy girl named Luna. She shared the school year with him, but he still spent the entirety of his summers exclusively with Niði. I'm not sure if she made much of an effort to steal his time away or not, but on very rare occasions, the three of them could be found together in the local library, or even at the local used bookstore, which Luna's father owned.

For the most part, Viktor was a normal child living a normal life, and what was normal for him just so happened to be a lot of arguing, a lot of hitting, and becoming the co-parent for his younger brother whether he wanted to or not. Viktor's father was very strict and as the eldest son, there was a lot of pressure placed on him to be the pinnacle of what a son *should* be. It was through this that I think he developed his sense of duty.

For the entire time that I've known him, Viktor has always piled a lot of responsibility on himself, but I often wished that he didn't. He never liked to show it, but I know it could really get overwhelming for him. I mean, I admire him to this day for his dependability and trustworthiness, of course, but I still wish he'd not take the load entirely on himself.

Oh, you know, I do know something that I haven't really mentioned yet. Viktor learned as a child that he had severe OCD and had been medicated for it as a result. I admit that I'd never met him before his diagnosis, so I may never know the full scope of just how much it's helped. However, he has confided in me that a lot of his obsessions ate him up inside and that unfortunately he never quite felt fully in control of himself either on or off medication. That conversation definitely came much later in life and there was much more to it than just that, but maybe this helps you understand him better. Maybe. I'm not sure. You might even know more about his condition than me.

Needless to say, his overall mental health was oft overlooked in his childhood, except for the one saving grace that was his medication, but he did his best. He's still doing his best. Like I said, he was a normal child living a normal life. His normal was just a little more stressful than the normal that exists for others.

I think that covers all I had to say about Viktor. It's Niði's turn now.

○ Niði

Niði Fiske was born in Oslo, Norway. A little more clueless than Viktor, he never even asked what his father did. His mother told him, when he was a young lad, that his father was a businessman and Niði accepted that as truth and didn't think to ask any other questions. It's interesting what children find important or unimportant, and you never really notice until it's too late for it to really matter, right?

In any case, his parents were married before they gave birth to Niði, and outside of his father constantly pestering him to toughen up, be a man, and go play outdoors, his relationship with them wasn't necessarily bad. He got along fairly well with his mother and did his best to respect his father. His parents might have tried for another child, but his mother became ill with some form of disease that took away her ability to do so. Niði never asked what the disease was, because he was a young child and didn't have the capacity to fully know that he probably could have asked, and it quickly became much too late for him to need to ask anymore.

But that's skipping ahead a little bit.

At age eight, he met Viktor over one of his usual summer trips to his grandmother's home, which was something Niði and his parents did every year since his birth. This tradition started because Niði's mother wanted *her* mother to be a part of her son's life. Unbeknownst to the young boy, his grandmother had always had frail health. Thus these yearly visits were an important mainstay in his life.

Meeting Viktor was a strong factor leading to Niði being excited for the summer season rather than dreading it. Not that he hated going, necessarily, but it took him a few years to really warm up to his grandmother. He warmed up to Viktor much faster. But outside of Viktor and their summers spent frolicking around the forests, Niði did what any other child did. He went to school. He excelled in school, too. It was as if learning was in his DNA; a real fish to water, as they say.

He was a fairly quiet and docile young man, apart from when he was with Viktor. As if his hobbies were meant to match his own light, wispy appearance, he was into soft things like reading and napping. He preferred curling up with a good book and a cracked open window, being left to his own devices for hours at a time, and staring at the clouds as they drifted past.

One of Niði's favorite hobbies was gardening with his mother on nice, warm days. Often in the evenings, he would settle in the grass with her and help tend to the soil. He learned much from her during these sessions and cherished the time they spent together. Rarely did he spend any sort of quality time with his father, so these backyard-gardening afternoons meant a lot to him.

His relationship with his family was normal, I think, for what many children experience. Though his tense relationship with his father would only sour further in the future, there was nothing terribly explosive about it. Some folks simply don't ever see eye to eye. This is as true of families as it is of friends, but in Niði's case, it really only ever applied to him and his family.

While not as duty-bound as his best friend, he still had his own neuroses and struggles with commitment and responsibility. Between his father's insistence in the boy learning useful skills, like firewood chopping and mild home repairs, and his mother's passive smiles, he was pressured towards certain habits that never quite inspired his heart. Additionally, Niði was just always a nervous little thing, a little shy, a little sensitive. He was more outwardly emotional than Viktor, but he didn't feel any more or less than him. Not necessarily. They just had different ways of expressing themselves and different methods of communication.

After years and years of being close friends, though, they would become very familiar with each other's feelings and methods of expression, and would be able to read each other better than most people would be able to read themselves.

But I'm getting ahead of myself again.

O Đ

I'll get back to the story, but I hope I've managed to fill in some of the gaps for now. If you have any other burning questions, then, well, I hope I answer them by the end. Anyway, there's a lot more to cover.

● Death and Spaghetti

Luckily and unluckily at the same time, once Niði hit age 15, his grandmother's health declined to such a degree that his parents decided to move in temporarily with the elderly woman. This was both in order for them to provide care and assistance to her as well as surround her with her family for what remained of her time.

Instead of just having a family trip over the summer, Niði and his family packed up shop and moved fully for what they knew might be an indeterminant amount of time. Nobody was quite sure if they had one year or three, but they hoped for the latter. Niði's family moved right as school ended for the season.

The silver lining that came of uprooting their lives to move to this town was that now Niði would be attending school with Viktor. Obviously, the already hormonal teen was feeling a little conflicted at this turn of events.

He mourned the coming loss of his grandmother, who he'd come to be very fond of in the recent years. But he would have been lying if he said he wasn't a little bit thrilled at the prospect of spending more than just two months of the year with his best friend, Viktor.

Now, this being a small town, the reputations surrounding the two of them continued to be about as unflattering as possible. Viktor's 'rabid dog' nickname stuck with him ever since his first outburst on the four goons and Niði was, of course, still under fire as well.

Naturally, this led to Viktor getting into fights nearly constantly with anyone who even so much as dared to open their mouths in Niði's direction. I know what you're thinking and maybe I could have phrased that better. I'm not trying to make Viktor sound like some sort of brutish thug, nor am I trying to make it sound like he wouldn't allow Niði to talk to other peers. I'm only trying to emphasize just how protective Viktor was of his delicate friend. And, for the most part, Niði was left alone outside of the occasional slur thrown his way from outside of Viktor's reach. Viktor really, sincerely, truly, did everything he could to make sure his best friend remained unscathed.

Regardless, only two years had passed since the first scuffle, but the stoic teen had found himself in numerous since. This too conflicted Niði, who didn't necessarily love seeing his friend getting hurt at all, and yet…he had to admit that there was something alluring about the idea of his friend defending him.

I think you'd be proud to know that Viktor was a very competent brawler. He never quite grew out of his viking phase, if you know what I mean. He was also the tallest kid in the town and seemed only to put on more and more muscle as the years went on, so the odds were certainly stacked in his favor. Concern for his wellbeing aside, Niði only feigned distress whenever Viktor got into spats on his behalf.

Anyway, it was time again for summer, and it was time for our awkward little teen to return to Viktor's home town. This time, he'd returned as a more permanent resident. Nearly as soon as he dropped his luggage in his allotted room, the very room he'd been using for the past seven years, which still never quite felt like his own but may as well have been at this point, he bolted out of the house to go find Viktor, who was waiting for him in their usual spot.

Once Niði rounded the corner and came face to face with Viktor, he waved a small greeting and called out to him cheerfully. "Hi Viktor!"

Then his dear friend did something he'd never seen him do before. He grinned. The blond nearly tripped over himself, stumbling to a stop. At first, Niði didn't know what he felt. He was so stunned by the sight of Viktor's beaming smile, that he couldn't possibly manage to process anything else.

Maybe it had been the gap in time since seeing him, or maybe it was the grin itself, but for the second time in his life, Niði felt like he was looking at his dark-haired friend for the first time. The blond was simply mesmerized.

All of Viktor's teeth were straight, except for one unruly incisor that had twisted itself into a crooked little snaggle-tooth, and his eyes had a way of vanishing behind his cheeks and under his heavy lids in a squint that reminded Niði very much of a cat. The surreal visual of his friend's bright grin was already enough to send Niði's head spinning, but the sound of Viktor's voice really sealed his fate.

"Hi Niði," he responded in a voice much lower than the smaller teen remembered. And Niði realized, as he regained some sense of locomotion and continued to close the gap between him and Viktor, that he might have to re-evaluate what his feelings for his friend were. But before he had much of a chance to get lost in those thoughts, he was hand in hand with him, already walking down the sidewalk towards their favorite hiding spot. With a bashful side-eye, Niði carefully examined his friend with a fresh perspective.

Niði himself hadn't changed as much, really. His hair was a little more well-managed than before, and his eyes were still silvery pale, but Viktor was decidedly and very definitely even taller somehow, and his hair had grown back out past the tops of his shoulders. He was a little broader, too. Built like a train. But, otherwise, he was probably not *that* much physically different than the previous year.

Once they were settled on their log in their usual spot, Viktor let go of his hand and looked up at the sky with a quiet sigh. Niði watched him for a few moments, just to see if he might have something to say, and when he didn't, then Niði decided to deliver his news.

"I'm going to be staying for the school year."

"Here?"

"Yeah. I'll be going to your school."

Viktor grinned again and Niði felt like his chest was being clamped down on by those pesky feelings that he hadn't yet had time to address.

"Hah, well…I mean, my parents and I are staying here for…" He trailed off and was faced with another mess of emotions in the entirely opposite direction. And then, without any further warning, he started to cry. In that very instant, he became so frustrated with himself for crying that he cried just a little harder.

Viktor wrapped his arms around him in a very warm and welcomed hug. Niði had absolutely no chance in the world to stop crying at this point, so he did what he had to. He let the tears come and go, riding out the worst of it in the privacy of their secret garden.

When he eventually calmed down and the silent stream became a little, shivering sniffle, he pulled away from Viktor enough to look up at him with a pathetic little frown. His friend reduced his embrace to a one-armed affair, holding the back of Niði's neck in a warm palm. He didn't seem interested in asking just what had caused the outburst, but the blond teen found the strength to confess, regardless.

He said, "My grandma is dying…She's only got, you know…She's not doing so well now."

"Oh…"

"Yeah…"

There wasn't much else to say about that, but still. Viktor scraped the bottom of the barrel and found something to offer, regardless. In a soft, very nearly imperceptible hum, he eventually said, "I'm glad that you're staying longer, though."

Much to his relief, I'm sure, Niði responded, "Me too." And that was that.

The next few days they spent together weren't nearly as emotionally draining as the first day of summer had been. That was a bit of a doozy for multiple reasons. For starters, it had been the first time that Niði had admitted out loud (in any capacity) that his beloved grandmother was very likely in her last few years. He confessed it to Viktor, because of course he did. He told Viktor everything. But he didn't say anything about it at all after that point.

Part of him didn't want to think about it. Another part of him wanted to focus on Viktor instead. And a different part of him was afraid that bringing it up too many times would bring it on more quickly. So he clammed up and left the conversation where it lie.

Instead, they filled their days with talks of their favorite books and the things they had read in each other's absence. As usual, Viktor had read some historical literature, books on the history of Scandinavia, the history of Iceland specifically, and even a few books about Finland and Canada. Meanwhile, Niði had branched out a little more into the world of fiction. Scientific books and non-fiction still captured his mind's lust for knowledge, but he was slowly discovering that getting lost in a good story was just as good.

"Do you have any books with you today, Vik?" Niði asked with little preamble. He had forgotten the collection of short-stories he was reading at home in his haste to meet up with his friend.

Viktor looked out at the trees in front of them, looked upward, then looked down at the ground before looking back at Niði. He nodded once.

"Read to me?" Niði's question was halfway a demand, and for some reason, this almost made Viktor smirk. Almost. But Niði could tell that he had in spirit.

From the interior pocket of his thin leather jacket, Viktor produced a small, old-looking paperback with a cover so faded and scuffed with wear and tear, that Niði had no clue what the book could possibly be. Not for lack of trying, though. Leaning over with his head tilted and neck stretched out, he tried to examine it before Viktor opened it to a seemingly random page. I promise, it wasn't a random page. Viktor simply didn't believe in bending the top corners of the pages of books (as any respectable human shouldn't), nor did he believe in bookmarks. He simply memorized the number of the page he stopped at every time he had to take a break from reading. More often than not, though, he just plowed through books in one sitting, often staying up well into the wee hours of the night to do so. It wasn't uncommon for him to be up until dawn reading, only to be found groggily ambling around the next day.

Regardless, he opened the book to the page he needed, took another quick look at the trees, the sky, and the ground, then read.

"Ég missti skálina með spaghettínu á flísalagt eldhúsgolfið. Skálin eyðilagðist og ég grét í þrjá tíma."

"Stop."

Even before Niði spoke up, Viktor had a stupid, tiny, hint of a smirk on his face.

"Viktor! That's not what the book says at *all*," the small blond whined before fixing him with as viciously stern a glare as he could muster.

"Ó jæja, fyrirgefðu," he apologized, stilling the laugh that struggled to shake itself from his chest. "You read it, then…You tell *me* what it says."

Niði's hard stare faltered into a wave of laughter, shattering the illusion of his ire in an instant. "I *can't* read that, but I'm *certain* there isn't anything about crying over spilled spaghetti in whatever this book is."

"…Is that all you caught from that?"

"Yeah," Niði responded before giving his shoulder a playful shove. "That was a tough one."

It was one of Viktor's favorite games to play with his dear friend. I'm not sure when exactly he picked up this habit, but at some point he'd decided it was more fun to pretend to read a book and see how far and how absurd he could get with his stories before Niði noticed. He'd been caught pretty easily this time, though the farthest he was able to go before was one full page-worth of rambling nonsense.

As much as Niði protested, it was his favorite game, too.

"So, what *is* this book about?" he asked, carefully and gently plucking the tattered old book from Viktor's hands.

"I'm not sure…Crying over spaghetti would be my first g—"

And the last attempt to convince Niði that this little old book, found somewhere in the furthest corner of an old bookshelf, was a heart-wrenching story about a man dropping his bowl of spaghetti was knocked away by one of Niði's elbows jabbing Viktor in the ribs.

With a deep breath, Viktor sighed out the last of his chuckles. "Alright. It's just an old book about all the different types of volcanic rocks you can find in Iceland, or something like that…I'm not too sure, actually. I haven't read very far and this author seems to take forever to get to the point."

"Huh? But, that sounds so interesting…" Niði responded with a wistful gaze at the yellowed pages of the little book. He flipped through it aimlessly, muttering a few of the words as they caught his eye. Viktor was watching Niði the whole time, but he pretended not to notice as the blond stumbled all over the tricky Icelandic words.

Without having to acknowledge him, Niði could sense that Viktor was struggling with his desires to immediately correct any pronunciation mishaps, but as long as the blond continued to ignore him, Viktor wouldn't jump in or say anything. Viktor only ever corrected Niði when asked to.

Casually, Niði changed course and slid into a slightly different topic. He said, "You still visit, right?"

"Visit?"

"Iceland. You visit Iceland, right?"

"Yeah, sometimes."

"Someday, I think I want to visit it, too. I want to go to Vik and see the black sand beach."

Viktor didn't respond immediately. He took a few extra moments to navigate the statement. It was still often very difficult for him to know what was being implied in moments like these. I know that his younger friend was trying to be honest and blunt, really, but he didn't really have the courage yet to say what he really wanted to, so he hid behind gentle, casual statements instead. He probably should have just told Viktor directly that he wanted to visit Iceland with *him* someday.

Recognizing this in himself, Niði pressed boldly onward, and followed up by saying, "Maybe we could go together."

"Okay."

It was decided, regardless of whether either of them knew how serious the other was.

O Ð

I don't think I remembered to emphasize just how strangely the pair were perceived by any of their peers. Outside of the bullying, for almost a decade, the two may as well have been a local attraction during the summer, based solely on the fact that they were as consistently observed as the season itself. Now, a casual onlooker might think that Viktor was the pushy one. He was the one that would grab Niði's hand and drag him around town, after all. He was quiet, which made everyone assume he was sulky. And he was always so blunt and bland whenever he did speak that it sounded a little as if he was bossing the poor kid around, too.

That was never the case.

In fact, it was always Niði that was in charge of the whole show, but I don't think he realized that for a very long time, you know? Try to remember that, though. Viktor was always bending to Niði's will. He was always trying to do what he thought Niði wanted, even if the blond didn't notice. So, in a weird way, all those dumb teenagers that called Viktor Niði's pet were sort of right.

Anyway, I think it's difficult, sometimes, to ever differentiate your perspective from someone else's. I also think it's hard to know what anyone ever really thinks of you, and thus it's kind of impossible to know if they're correct or not. It's really, really difficult to ever know if you or anyone else have the same viewpoints at all.

When I met that friend for lunch and had that super awful conversation with her, I learned a lot about perspective. I don't actually think she was intending any serious harm when she did what she did or said what she said, but what she did was still very wrong and the way she went about it was just terrible. I still hold it against her and I'm not sure I can forgive her. I've tried very hard to look at things from her point of view, but no matter how I try to wrap my head around it, I just come out hurt and confused.

You know what? I actually *do* think she intended to cause me direct harm, but I don't think she understood just how badly it would hurt me. Oh well. Such is life.

I try to be empathetic whenever I can, but this is just one of those instances where I can't be. I just can't.

I can forgive obnoxious teenagers for bullying Viktor and Niði. They were young and a little ridiculous. Everyone is sort of a terrible person at that age, but not out of malice. It's just a tough age to be and it's difficult to know what kind of person you want to be or why. I'm sure they grew up to learn from their mistakes. At least, that's what I want to believe. I choose to believe that.

But my friend—well, I shouldn't even be calling her a friend, that's too much credit for what we are now—I don't understand why she did what she did. I don't understand her reasoning. I can't see it from her perspective and I probably never will.

● Time is a Responsibility

Viktor spent every possible waking moment with Niði, even once school was back in session. Sure, the surly teen had made one whole other friend, the artistic girl I mentioned earlier. Luna. Sometimes, she was actually seen together with both Niði and Viktor, but not nearly so often as she might have liked. I don't know. I never knew her that well, so I can't say for certain, but it *felt* like she wanted to be around them more.

In contrast with the very pragmatic and historical interests that encompassed Viktor, Luna liked everything whimsical and fantasy-oriented. She was a painter, though I'm not sure I have a good enough eye for that sort of thing to be able to tell you if she was a very good painter or not. She sculpted, too. I think she even danced, though I'm not sure if it was a type of ballroom or ballet. I just remember thinking she was a dancer. It might have been the graceful nature of her movements, or her petite frame, but something about her just screamed *dancer*.

Her father owned the local bookstore, as I've mentioned before. That's initially what got her and Viktor on speaking terms in the first place. I don't know who saw whom first, if it was Viktor that approached her or the other way around, but it had made Niði very happy that Viktor had made at least one other friend.

Luna talked about birds and pictures, films and paintings. All the sorts of things that Viktor knew next to nothing about. He listened politely in his own silent way, and she rambled on about whatever drifted to her mind from the sea of consciousness.

"So have you guys ever been swimming in the ocean? I'm too afraid of it, myself." Luna always started conversations with a question, and she always made sure to include both Niði and Viktor in her initial reports, but she'd inevitably end up drifting closer and closer to just Viktor and Niði would end up sidelined to watch them. This never really bothered him, of course. I just think Viktor was always her goal and Niði was too much of a wallflower to impose too much on their conversations otherwise.

Viktor gave her very little in response. He almost never responded to her, so I'm not sure why she was so keen on talking to him. Most folks would rather share a conversation with someone that was a little less one-sided than the little chats she navigated with Viktor, so it seemed a bit odd that she remained so persistent with him. I can't say that I blame her, though. Viktor, once you noticed him, had a certain mysterious charm. To me, at least. And maybe to Luna, too.

The three of them spent a decent amount of time together at the bookstore, with Luna's father absolutely thrilled that the teens were there instead of causing mischief elsewhere, as so many young hooligans were prone to do. In his opinion, everyone should love reading and share that love with each other in every way possible.

I don't actually think Luna *did* like reading, but she definitely liked Viktor.

Anyway, her father, Erkki, a kind old pudgy man with a bristly mustache and long, balding hair sometimes joined the trio to chat about the latest magazine releases. Niði adored talking with him and most of his fledgling love for fiction literature took flight because of him. As they lingered there, the little table would be invisibly divided between the young blond chatting with the older man and the short girl desperately trying to squeeze more than one word at a time out of the taciturn teen.

Though sometimes Viktor would get overwhelmed with the noise of too many overlapping voices and, without a word, he'd get up, tap Niði's shoulder, and leave. Niði, with an apologetic little flourish, would nearly immediately get up and follow him. Erkki, who had seen all kinds and worked with children his whole life, always seemed to understand and never found Viktor's abrupt departures rude. But I think it slowly chipped away at Luna's patience. She wanted to be friends so badly, and it seemed as though the older boy just didn't care.

He *did* care, honest.

He just often got overwhelmed by various chaotic sounds and voices. He preferred quiet, one-on-one conversations and struggled a little in groups. Anything that pushed him into wider social situations always seemed to irritate him a little. But Niði could tell by the way

Viktor nodded his head in response to Luna's rambling that he really was trying to be an attentive listener. It didn't seem as though he disliked her.

Whatever she felt, Luna never followed when Viktor left. She probably could have, and I don't think Niði or Viktor would have minded too terribly, but she never did and I don't know why she didn't.

After the two boys made their escape from the bookstore, they would wander around a little, usually until the taller boy found a quiet spot to sit, like a park bench or their secret log-garden. Once they were seated again, Niði knew it was safe to talk.

"Are you okay?" He always liked to check in with Viktor, even though the answer never changed.

"Are *you* okay?" Viktor almost always repeated the question back.

"Yeah."

"Okay. Me too."

And so it went.

As I've already mentioned, navigating the turbulent seas of adolescence was a bit of a challenge for Niði. Perhaps it was a holdover from his frowned-upon friendship with Viktor, or maybe his own timid nature, but he struggled to find friends and fit in with anyone else in the school. During classes with groupwork, Niði was consistently the last person to find a group. He was a little too shy to join any of his peers unprompted and often had to be assigned a group by the teacher.

He dreaded those situations. Niði much preferred sitting quietly aside and doing his classwork solo, for he never felt that his peers clicked with him and it was usually easier to just work through assignments on his own.

Often, he wished that Viktor was the same age as him so that they could be in the same class. Niði certainly wouldn't have minded working with Viktor. He wouldn't have minded working with Luna, either.

But, alas, the poor blond was alone in a little pod of distant peers. He was very much so just the shy, quiet kid who sat at the edge of the group while the others around him buzzed and chatted away.

"Niði?" One of his groupmates, a mousy, blonde girl asked him from across the table.

A little startled from his thoughts, Niði bolted straight upright, lifted his chin from his palm and slapped his hand on the table. "Yes!?"

The girl jumped and gave him a peculiar look. Niði felt himself shrink under her scrutiny. "What did you get for the third one?"

"Third one?"

Now, his other groupmate, a curly-haired boy, gave Niði a crooked look. Tacking onto the girl's question, he said, "The third question on the assignment. What did you get for it?"

"Oh! Sorry," Niði responded, a little embarrassed. He had been so lost in his daydreaming that he hadn't even gotten past the first question. "I haven't done that one yet."

"Oh," the girl responded.

With that, Niði's groupmates took it upon themselves to solve that particular question themselves, leaving Niði entirely on his own. The curly boy and the mousy girl continued to chat about the answers amongst themselves and Niði trailed after them with penciled scratchings of notes. As expected, neither of his groupmates asked him for his input for the remainder of class. So he sat quietly with a pleasantly vacant smile until the school day ended.

Once he was free to do so, Niði gathered his things and rushed out of the room. After the awkward group study, he was eager to leave school to find Viktor. This was easy to accomplish, since Viktor was waiting in the usual spot as always. Luna joined them soon after.

The three of them walked to the park, following Viktor's lead out of habit. Niði vented his frustrations for the day and the others listened. As it turned out, Luna had her own complaints about her classes. Together, the little blond and she engaged in whiny catharsis, with Viktor quietly listening in.

"I just wish I wasn't the last person to find a group every time, you know?"

"And I just wish Andra would stop bothering me about her stupid lipstick."

Niði leaned forward to look past Viktor at Luna. "Huh?"

Luna shrugged and pinched a stray hair between her fingers. "I dunno. She wants to know if I think Best notices it or not."

"The lipstick?"

"Yeah."

"...Did Best notice?"

"How should I know?" she responded with a groan. "Ask Best."

Without knowing how to respond, Niði leaned back against the bench and sighed. He had no idea who Best or Andra was, nor what the significance of lipstick might be. Meeting Viktor's eyes, Niði tilted his head in a silent question. Viktor smiled minutely and shrugged a shoulder.

Luna huffed a sigh.

"Anyway," Niði said, "I don't have any friends in any of my classes…"

"So?" Luna's voice dragged a little.

"So…?"

Luna huffed another quick sigh. Focusing on the strand of hair twined between her fingers, she asked, "What do you want to do about it?"

"Well, I dunno…"

"And you're pissed off because you're always picked last or whatever?"

"I guess, yeah," Niði responded, though he wasn't sure that 'pissed off' was the right descriptor.

"Why don't you just ask someone to group up with you first?" She suggested flatly, "I mean, it's not that big of a deal."

Niði glanced at Viktor, who nodded slowly.

So the next time his class demanded for groupwork, Niði followed his friend's advice and tried to be proactive. He crushed down his anxieties, stood up, and approached the first pair of classmates that caught his eye: a tall, dark-haired girl and a shorter girl with thin eyes.

"Hi," he started nervously. Already, Niði could feel the pressure of their stares. They seemed to be a little offended that he approached them, given their aloof expressions. That wasn't going to deter Niði. He continued, "Could I join your group?"

"Actually, no," the dark-haired girl responded with a quick sigh.

"Sorry, we already asked Emma to be in our group," the thin-eyed girl quickly added. Her eyes darted around the room a little as she spoke and Niði found himself looking around with her.

He mumbled a small response, saying softly, "Oh."

As he turned away, so did the pair of girls, but the thin-eyed girl spoke over her shoulder, "Maybe Erik still needs a partner?" before fully turning her back on Niði. They giggled and exchanged a few low whispers amongst themselves and Niði's cheeks burned in response. It was embarrassing enough to be rejected, but the tittering of their lowered voices just added to the humiliation of the whole affair.

He didn't even bother trying to ask Erik whether or not he could join his group, being too disheartened to face another rejection. Eventually, the teacher assigned him to a group and the rest of the school day passed by in a dull greyscale.

You know what? I've forgotten something, and I think it's important.

When Viktor and Niði were 11 and 9 respectively, they found a dead bird while roaming the forest. When the dark-haired boy saw it, he broke down into tears and sobs that would rival the smaller boy's greatest meltdowns. I mean it. Viktor was really inconsolable.

The sight of this bird caused such tangible anguish, that little Niði had absolutely no clue how to react, nor how to comfort his friend. He started crying too, out of empathetic response. This was the first time that Niði took Viktor's hand first and was the one to guide him away.

Even out of sight of the bird, the older boy continued to sniffle and cry for a good long while. He never told Niði why. I'm not sure to this day why the bird made him cry so fiercely. It just sticks out to me as significant. For all of Niði's time with him, he had only ever seen Viktor cry three times, and this was the first time.

Once he calmed down, Viktor told Niði that seeing a dead creature simply made him sad. He provided no further elaboration and the conversation ended there.

Alright, so Niði's first year of school with Viktor was a little rough at times, but the older teen always made sure to keep most of their antagonizers at bay. This was the age of schoolkids that often made for cruel and unruly folk and, needless to say, our shy hero was an easy target.

Though he would never blame Viktor for this, part of the reason he was ridiculed *was* because he spent so much time gallivanting around town, holding Viktor's hand and exclusively spending his time with the known troublemaker. Another large portion of the reason he was tormented was simply because he was delicate, soft-spoken, and timid. The four great goons and their posse of friends were always the most vehement of tormentors, but being a small town, they composed a significant slice of Niði's social circle.

Though, for the most part, outside of a few sideways snickers from the occasional straggler, it really was mostly just the rowdy four and a handful of their contemporaries that bothered Niði. Mostly everyone else was either indifferent, too busy with their own social lives, or afraid of Viktor. A lot of the other kids were afraid of Viktor, actually. I suppose that's one of the perks of being best friends with the big, scary, quiet kid.

And Viktor was just that. He was big, not only in height, but also in sheer density. At a glance, if you didn't know him, you might have thought he was well entrenched in the world of athleticism and sports. He wasn't necessarily, but he did spend a lot of time working hard with his father and enjoyed the nightly trip to the gym for healthy exercise. He was just about the tallest 17-year-old anyone had ever seen, and he wore a lot of red and black (still does). Usually, a black shirt with a dark red flannel or something. I guess you could say he looked like he was big into the grunge-rock scene, which he was. Niði, by comparison, was average in height, but standing next to Viktor made him seem smaller than he was. He was also fairly trim and had a little bit of lean muscle from his time spent working on chores with his father, but was nowhere near as toned as Viktor. With fair, freckled skin and a particular fondness for light shades of purple, Niði looked to be Viktor's opposite. Tall, dark, and aloof meets small, soft, and shy.

By now, nearly all of their peers in the town thought of them as the 'weirdo queers' or, more popularly, 'the fag and his rabid dog', but the physical bullying had subsided a little bit. Nobody had the courage to call Viktor a 'fag' to his face and they certainly had the right idea to fear him, because he most definitely would have punched them without hesitation. They had a little less reservation in the matter when it came to Niði, who all too aggressively denied any accusation and was brought to tears every time.

However, the folks that found enjoyment in Niði's suffering still feared Viktor and were not nearly as likely to bother the smaller teen while they were together. Like I said, being best friends with the big teen had its perks here and there. So while the verbal jabs were still present, and someone might attempt to shoulder shove the poor lad here and there, for the most part his time at school was relatively peaceful.

I don't really have much to say about their teen years regarding school life. What do you remember most about school? Classwork was either engaging or boring, depending on the topic, and you probably spent time trying to stay awake in class or hanging out with your friends. This was largely the same for the two young lads.

Both Niði and Viktor had varying degrees of interest in what they learned, and they both maintained their grades as well as you'd expect of the two studious fellows. Neither of them were interested in making any friends outside of each other, save for Luna and her persistence, and you already know that they weren't very popular outside of that. What else? They spent time together in the bookstore, the library, the park, the forest, though never at each other's houses. Sometimes they'd end up in Luna's home, having been invited over for board games and dinner by Erkki. Those nights were cozy, but they didn't stand out terribly too much in Niði's mind.

As you may expect from the blond boy, he dreaded physical education classes like the plague, and he hated having to change clothes in the locker room in front of the others. When possible, he weaseled his way out of the class, or changed in a bathroom stall instead. Sports were never something he was interested in and the locker room was a terrible, vile, awful place to be for a young boy being tormented over his frailty. Niði hated any sort of gym class.

Not only was he targeted in the changing rooms, but also in the games they played in the class as well. Balls were hurled at him, kids would 'accidentally' run into him, and other such things. It was all very uncouth and the blond hated these classes more than he hated anything else in his life at this point. In fact, he hated them so much that all he wanted to do was scream and kick and lash out. Take a page out of Viktor's book. Anything to end the torment, really. But unfortunately, little Niði didn't quite have the courage to stand up for himself or enact any warranted revenge.

So let's just gloss over that and let it go for now.

I'm still struggling for things to describe here, though. You might even know more than me, anyway. At least, about this period of Viktor's life. Maybe.

Oh, you know who we haven't talked about that much, yet? Aleksi.

As I mentioned before, Viktor and his family moved to Norway because Viktor's father's girlfriend wanted to move here after having her son. Viktor was often relegated to babysitter status nearly every evening, when both his father and his father's girlfriend were out of the house.

He did his best. As good as any kid his age could have. However, this did put quite the damper on their relationship, so to speak. But as far as Viktor was concerned, becoming his brother's third parent wasn't such a bad thing. Responsibly-minded and of a helpful nature, he really didn't mind taking care of Aleksi when it was required of him. It was a matter of logic and duty. He was the elder brother, their guardians were frequently absent, and this was the most reasonable thing to do.

Though, to say that raising Aleksi was a labor of love might be giving a little too much credit to Viktor. It really was more about pragmatism rather than compassion. From Aleksi's perspective, Viktor was far, far too bossy for his liking. I wouldn't know the details, and I've only had the chance to meet Aleksi a handful of times, so I can't speak too confidently about his feelings, but his and Viktor's relationship was strained. A large reason for that was Viktor's forced parentage upon him. He was probably too young to be able to put these feelings into words at the time, but the younger brother really just wanted, well, a brother. Not another father. A brother. And that wasn't what Viktor was acting like.

The first time Niði ever actually met Aleksi was the year before his family moved more permanently into his grandmother's home. He'd caught glimpses of him before, but never had the chance to make any introductions. The day he met the younger brother stood out to him, though, just because looking at the kid was a little like looking back through time to a younger Viktor. It was startling just how similarly the two resembled each other.

But the longer Niði looked, the more differences he saw between them. Viktor's jaw was broader. More defined. Aleksi's came to a fine point. His face was a little more pinched than Viktor's, and the expressions he wore on his face were far too intense to bear much of a resemblance to Viktor's subtle ones. They were undeniably related, though. Years later, to my shock, Viktor told me that he had a different mother from Aleksi. It was a woman neither boy had ever had the chance to meet, but the brothers still turned out looking as if they could have been twins. What struck Niði the most was how both Viktor and Aleksi had the same stormy-blue colored eyes.

The day Niði officially met Aleksi, Niði was 14, Viktor 16, and his younger brother 10. Viktor had brought Aleksi along to go to the bookstore. It was a simple act of kindness, because at this point in his life, the younger brother would rather be home alone watching television and Viktor thought he'd try to bring him out for a little fun. Aleksi had asserted that he was old enough to be on his own without Viktor's hovering, but Viktor genuinely wanted to try to do something nice. He wanted to share the gift of reading with his brother.

Unfortunately, Aleksi wasn't having it.

"I'm going home," he announced, right as the three of them reached the block the bookstore was on.

"No," Viktor responded after looking up at the sky, then at the ground, and back towards the front. His voice was firm, making it difficult to argue with him.

"I know which bus to take, so I'm going home. I'm tired of walking around and I don't care about books," his argument was abrupt and choppy. In a way, it reminded Niði a little bit of Viktor's own style of arguing, but it was too verbose to really suit the older brother.

"We're almost there."

"Do you like to read, Aleksi?" Niði wanted to try to break the tension, maybe provide a distraction, help Viktor co-debate, if possible. Anything.

Peering over Aleksi's head, Viktor looked at his blond friend with a nearly unreadable expression. He didn't say anything out loud, but the slight downward tilt of his mouth said, "This is my problem. You don't have to worry about it."

Niði shrugged in response.

Then Aleksi said, "No. It's boring."

"That's just because you haven't found the right book yet," the blond countered with a smile. "What kind of shows do you like to watch, then?"

"I dunno."

Viktor sighed. Niði looked up at him sympathetically.

"Well," the blond said as cheerfully as possible. "We'll find something for you, anyway, okay?"

Aleksi sighed too. Some of the brothers' habits were laughably similar, despite their obvious differences. Niði found this dichotomy to be fascinating. Seeing Viktor interact with *anyone* else was fascinating on its own, but catching a tiny glimpse of his family dynamics was an entirely new world.

"I want to go home," the mini-Viktor complained, right at the door to the shop.

"No," his older brother shot down as he pulled open the door and stomped inside.

Aleksi followed petulantly, and Niði trailed after, unable to resist the tug of a smile at the side of his mouth. The brotherly dispute was a little endearing, for it was something he'd never experienced. I'm sure Niði would understand better his best friend's exasperation were he to have his own little brother. Perhaps. But, alas.

Once they were in Erkki's fine establishment, the quarreling ceased. This was due in large part to wise old Erkki's excellence at managing moody children. I don't remember exactly what was said, nor do I remember how it was said, but the man had a way with kids that transcends any skill I've ever known.

Thanks to Erkki's guidance, Aleksi was indeed able to find a suitable book and was quietly stuffed against a comfortable armchair reading it. Viktor was sitting within eyesight, but far enough away to give the kid space. He sat at a little, round table with Niði. He wasn't in a talkative mood right now, but the blond could tell that he was feeling considerably better about the situation with his brother. If anything, it was quiet and peaceful, and that's all Viktor ever wanted.

"You cooped up with those books again, Niði?" From down the hall, his father called to him.

Niði, who had been admiring his stash of pressed flowers, suddenly found himself scrambling to hide everything on his desk. Little bracelets and woven braids were carefully, but fervently, gathered and crammed between the pages of the inconspicuous novel splayed open before him. All his treasured floral gifts that Viktor had repeatedly made for him over the years, every little one that Niði managed to keep secret from his father, were quickly re-homed between whatever random pages he flipped to.

He just managed to slam the thing shut just before father entered the room.

"You finish weeding the garden yet?"

This was a trick question. They so often were with his father. They both knew that Niði had not, in fact, finished weeding the garden. Still, the young blond didn't want to just ignore his father. That wasn't often the best course of action, but as he stared up at him, Niði's mind went blank. Unfortunately, his silence dragged too long and his father's tone tilted in a strained direction.

"You got all the time in the world to be hiding in these books, and none to help your grandma in the garden?"

Trick question after trick question. Silently rising from his desk, Niði couldn't bear to make eye contact with his father. Niði was a field mouse before an adder. One false move, one false answer, and he'd face the full force of his father's scolding.

"Bring that to me."

Never before had Niði's blood run so cold.

"Bring me that book, Niði."

His father must've caught him. The little blond wasn't as quick as he thought he was.

Obediently, Niði did as he was told, regardless of how uncomfortable and unhappy this made him. The short few steps to his father stood out to him in how painfully aware he was in the texture of the rug beneath his socked feet, the way his vision seemed to tunnel in and shimmer at the edges of his sight. If there was one thing in the world that Niði didn't want to do in this moment, it was handing this book and its flowery secrets to his dad. But he did it anyway. He had to.

After letting go of it, Niði stared at the book and watched mortified as his father flipped brazenly through it. Since the flowers were so haphazardly shuffled between the pages, they quickly tumbled out from their hiding places and fell to the floor.

For an ungodly amount of time, Niði stared cherry-faced and seasick as his father unceremoniously flapped through the book with an impassive expression. Eventually, he asked the blond, "What is this?"

"They're just flowers from the garden," Niði lied.

"That so?"

Niði faltered after making the critical mistake of glancing at his father. The split-second hesitation before he responded wasn't unnoticed. "Yes."

The man narrowed his eyes at his son and tossed the book aside. The boy winced as the poor thing clattered down. He said, "Then, that's where they should stay. Quit fucking around with flowers and act your age."

"Okay." There was no way he could argue. The situation would only explode if he were to do that.

His father glared at him. Niði wasn't out of the clear yet. "Get it together. You can't keep living with your head in the clouds playing around in the flowers. Understand? You need to live in the real world."

Ignoring how contradictory it felt for his father to both tell him to go work in the garden and also not play with flowers, Niði simply responded, "Okay."

"You think I'm stupid?"

Niði's eyes jerked up to meet his father's. "What?"

"Is 'okay' the only word you know?"

Definitely not for the first time during the conversation, Niði felt it would be impossible to answer the question. This was a total failure situation. He made the mistake of answering anyway. "No."

"Excuse me?" His father's words hissed.

"I know more words," Niði mumbled indignantly, his defiance teetering between meek submission and fed-up outburst.

"You must really think I'm stupid. That right, boy?"

Sullen, but too afraid of his father's wrath, Niði replied, "No."

"No?"

"No, sir."

"That's right."

Mercifully, his father sighed and shook his head rather than push Niði into a full-blown argument. He gave one last stern stare, then said, "Get rid of the flowers, boy, then finish your chores."

Shame and rage stirred around in Niði's stomach. He was sick of being treated like everyone's doormat. That his hobbies and interests—his beloved treasures from Viktor—were constantly under threat of discovery and judgment made his head spin countless fantasies. He dreamed up billions of scenarios where he was the one to come out on top. For once.

O Đ

I went to university for a long while. I wasn't entirely certain what I wanted to do with my life, so starting that journey was a little daunting, as you might imagine. Did you ever go to university? Did you ever pursue any higher education? I don't think it's for everyone, and I don't think we should force folks into it that aren't prepared or willing.

In hindsight, I'm glad I went, but it was a rough first few years. For starters, I was far away from my hometown, and that was tough. I didn't yet know what I even wanted to go to school for, so that didn't make it any easier. But just as with most things in life, I eventually found my way. Viktor went to university, too, you know? His brother didn't, but I think he found a good path for himself to be on in the end.

When I was young and hadn't yet figured myself out, I thought that I might like to open a little cafe. A specialty cafe, though. Perhaps a bookstore-cafe combo, or a cafe for writing supplies. Finding a good notebook can always be such a hassle, you know? Imagine a cafe where you can find a good notebook and enjoy a nice cup of coffee. Or a particularly smooth fountain pen and some lovely tea. A safe haven for those who enjoy quiet and stories. That was one of my more grandiose dreams, but as I got further and further in my studies at university, I learned that I had entirely different goals than the ones I thought I had.

Does that make sense?

I think it does. I think it takes a lot more insight than anyone expects to know what you want to do with your life. I don't know if anyone ever actually finds that answer or if they just stumble upon their dreams as they drift through life. Did your aspirations sneak up on you like mine did to me?

I know of only one person that ever knew with certainty exactly what he wanted to be, and that was Viktor. Can you guess what he wanted to do with his life?

● A Proposal

Viktor wanted to be a father. He confessed this to Niði right after his 18th birthday. The proclamation came out of nowhere, as did most of Viktor's conversation starters, and it was such an unexpected thing for him to say that his friend laughed a little in response. This earned a curious frown from the dark-haired fellow.

"No, no, I'm not laughing at you, I'm sorry. I just didn't expect you to say that. It surprised me, that's all," Niði said quickly with a sheepish grin.

Viktor looked up, left, back at his friend, back at the sky. It took him a little longer than usual to complete his little ritual, but once he'd set his eyes back on Niði, he said, "I just want to have a kid someday."

"I think…That sounds nice, right? I don't think I've ever thought about it. I guess I'd like to get married to someone nice someday. Maybe we'll have kids. I dunno." As he spoke, his face scrunched a little in thought. Viktor's eyes could bore holes into him.

"I think I want to get married, too."

Niði smiled a little and shifted a little against the park bench. There just so happened to be a pair of parents playing with a little child in the grass a distance away from them. He wondered if seeing them was what triggered the thought to spring from Viktor's mind. Maybe so.

"Who do you want to marry, Vik?"

Niði should have known that this was a dangerous question to ask. His dear friend had a tendency to switch into oddly mischievous moods at the slightest provocation, and what seemed to be a perfectly innocent question turned out to be an embarrassing (but endearing) trip down memory lane.

"Well, actually," he started as a flicker of a smile twisted at the corner of his lips. "Remember when we were kids...?"

On the immediate—but equally playful—defensive, Niði responded, "Of course I remember when we were kids."

"No. Remember? We're already married."

"What?!" The poor lad's mind scrambled as he tried to rifle through the cobwebs of his mind to find what memory specifically he should conjure to make sense of what Viktor had said. A nervous knot tugged at his chest.

"*Jæja*...Have you forgotten?"

"No!?" Niði lied in a panic.

Viktor then beamed a devilish grin in his friend's direction.

Niði's heart skittered and pounded in response. Viktor's grin. A rare sight. Something that never failed to fluster the boy. He still couldn't figure out what his friend was talking about. I mean, especially not now. Not when Viktor was looking at him *like that*.

"It was the third summer we spent together...I wrote you that saga in the dirt with that stick I found at the pond. Remember?"

"Oh, yeah! When we got lost behind the school!" The dawning realization struck Niði and he laughed brightly as the events replayed in his mind. The memory crept upon him with little flashes here and there.

"I wrote that I was going to take land, and you were my wife, and we had a son that we named Eirikr, and he was going to be...*efniligr maðr*."

The smaller blond laughed and grinned at the silly memory. "But, why did I have to be the wife?"

"They don't talk about husbands as much in sagas," he responded quietly. After a few more seconds of thought, he continued. "It's usually, 'this guy was son of this guy, who was friends with this other guy. He had a wife and they had this land. This was their son.' Things like that. I don't think I knew the word then, is all..." As Viktor explained, the ghost of his sneaky smirk still endured in his crinkled eyes.

"Alright, then. So, what's the word? Do you know it now?"

"Yes. I know it."

"What is it?"

"I'm not telling you." That blinding grin, the crooked tooth, the way his lips stretched. Niði's feeble heart skyrocketed into his throat again.

"Viktor! Why not?"

"Wife, husband. It doesn't really matter. That's all." He'd said it with such finality, and while still making *that* particular smile, that Niði was stunlocked out of a response. He couldn't even begin to understand why Viktor had said such a thing. "Except, we don't have to have a son. It can be a daughter, too. I don't mind. I just want to be a parent," Viktor continued, tapping a finger on the bench as the smile faded from his face.

"O-okay…" Niði squeaked out, his face reddening with the conversation. Seeking an escape, he tried to look away from Viktor and instead found himself caught looking over at the family playing in the grass. He tried his hand at picturing himself and Viktor in their places.

Niði's face burned. Viktor might have even huffed a laugh. Or maybe he sneezed. It was a little unclear. I think it was around then that Viktor decided his little friend really *was* his betrothed. That Niði belonged with him. As with everything else the stormy-eyed lad said, he'd meant every word. This was surely no different. But the blond didn't fully realize yet how strong Viktor's feelings were.

Do you remember your first kiss? Your first love? Experiencing things for the first time tends to be some sort of rite of passage, depending on the thing in question. There are some firsts that a lot of people probably regret. That old saying, "there's a first time for everything" really drives me crazy. I probably just spend too much time thinking about it, but I strongly believe that there doesn't *need* to be a first time for some things.

I experienced plantar fasciitis for the first time a few years ago. Terrible. I wish I didn't know what that felt like. When I was a young adult, I experienced my first heartbreak. Gosh, that is a feeling I wish I could never, ever have experienced. I think I turned out fine, either way, but it really was rather unpleasant. There's that other saying, too, you know? "Time heals all wounds". That can be true, but I don't think some pains ever fully go away.

You see, the wound may be healed, but the regret is still there. Maybe I'm just too sensitive. What do you think?

Well anyway, I remember my first kiss clear as day. I remember my first love. The first time I realized I was in love. My first time traveling outside the country...My first time in a new school. There are a lot of good 'firsts' in the world, don't you think? I try to focus on those memories when I'm having a bad day. I think remembering things is pretty important, after all. That's the whole point I'm trying to make, isn't it?

I hope that I can share with you some of these memories and I hope they make you happy, too.

⬤ Just to Try

If you hadn't noticed, Viktor was never the type of person to question his identity. He was keenly aware of himself and who he was even at a young age.

Sure, he grew as a person and learned to appreciate certain aspects of himself, but he never doubted who he was as a person. He never went through that kind of teenage angst.

It might be applicable to say that parts of himself, be it his aversion to noise, his special interest in Icelandic sagas, or his love for Niði would all just creep up on him. He'd notice one day out of the blue, and maybe think or say out loud to himself, "Ah, that's the kind of person I am after all." And he'd accept those parts of himself, then and there, whenever he noticed them. So, I think he knew a little earlier on in his teen years the direction his feelings towards his beloved friend were turning, but it took a little more time with Niði.

And it makes sense, really. Any time Viktor had a surge of feelings or thoughts, he was often alone. He had plenty of time to sit and stew in his feelings and really navigate through them until he came to a conclusion. He did this with his words as much as he did this with his thoughts. He didn't have anyone to guide him or pressure him one way or another. He simply just thought and thought and thought until he figured something out.

Niði, on the other hand, was under constant pressure over his identity. He had to struggle between his own identity desires as well as the overbearing identity demands of his father. His father wasn't necessarily a terrible person, but he just had very specific ideas for a what a man should be and how his son should grow up to fit that mold.

Unfortunately, Niði didn't agree with those ideals. He wanted what everyone ultimately wants, to be himself.

Of course, his father wasn't the only problem here. The village goons sure had their way of making the young blond second-guess himself at every turn. How could Niði possibly accept his own feelings when they were used as weapons against him?

So that's how it came to be that Viktor was perfectly content and comfortable with his very obvious adoration for Niði and yet Niði himself had to take a little more time to reach the same conclusion. He was a little younger and a little more unsure of himself. It took a little longer for him to realize his feelings, but not too much longer.

One day, when Viktor was around 17, after school ended for the day, he was standing near the corner where he always stood. Waiting for Niði. As usual. Luna was with him, too.

"Did you know that Julia has a crush on you?"

Viktor didn't respond.

"Why don't you ask her to be your girlfriend?"

"...Why would I?"

Luna laughed. Her voice was so pretty and light, like a songbird. The tall teen didn't know why she was laughing. The correlation between Julia having a crush on him and him asking her out confused him. It simply didn't make sense for him to do something just on account of her feelings. "I don't like her. Why would I want to date her?"

"Because she's cute and she likes you, stupid. Have you ever had a girlfriend?"

Viktor frowned. Well, as much as he ever did, I suppose. He said, "No, I haven't."

It was around then that Niði trotted up to join them on the corner. For some reason, the sun was seemingly extra glaring and the chill on the breeze a little too piercing. He shivered as he waved a small greeting to the pair. "Hey!"

"Niði..." Viktor started. It looked like he was going to say something else, but Luna cut him off excitedly.

Her green eyes practically sparkled as she smiled at Niði. "Hey, have *you* ever had a girlfriend?"

I don't think Luna noticed, but Niði definitely did. Viktor's eyes shot around the sky and their surroundings two times over before he landed on his blond friend's face with intent attention.

"No...?" he responded, a little caught off guard by Viktor's stare and Luna's overzealous question.

Viktor looked away again.

"So…" She giggled a little and Viktor frowned at her instead.

"So what?" he asked flatly.

Something about the possible directions the conversation was turning was starting to make Niði's stomach ache. He very suddenly wished he wasn't there right then, but he couldn't escape now.

"So you've never kissed anyone, then? Really?" Luna practically vibrated with haughty joy. The way her mousy hair framed her face made her look like a coy weeping willow.

Niði released a breath he didn't realize he'd been holding.

"So?" Viktor still didn't understand the point of this conversation. He'd never had a girlfriend and he'd never kissed. Those weren't the sorts of things that mattered to him and, by his bland tone and flat expression, this was *very* apparent to his blond friend.

"Maybe you should try!"

Viktor frowned again and looked at the sky.

Luna looked a little put out by the non-answer. She opened her mouth, no doubt to say something else obnoxious, but this time Viktor cut her off.

"I'm leaving. Come on, Niði."

That was that. He turned and started walking, leaving Luna to pout after him. Obediently, Niði chased after him, relieved to be on his way. Something about Luna always made him a little uneasy, but he always chalked it up to her invasive, probing attitude. After all, Viktor still tolerated her, so surely she couldn't be a bad person.

But when they reached their secret garden—you know the one, the one with the toppled-over log—Viktor still seemed to have the previous conversation on his mind.

"Is it bad that I've never kissed anyone?" he asked with a tilt of his head.

Niði shook his head quickly.

Still as a stone, sitting next to Niði on the log, the dark-haired teen's eyes stared ahead as he remained deafeningly silent. He was deep in thought. His friend knew him well enough to stay just as quiet and wait until Viktor's mind made itself up. It took a while, a lot longer than usual, even for Viktor.

But eventually, his still frame thawed and he slowly shifted himself to face Niði. Their knees touched. For some reason, this made the smaller teen's heart leap into his throat. With a completely unreadable expression, Viktor asked, "Do *you* think we should try?"

"Try what?" Niði knew exactly what, but he needed a little more information from his friend before answering. His heart sped around his ribs as he struggled to stay calm under Viktor's stare.

To Niði's relief, Viktor also seemed to be a bit nervous, given that he did a cycle of staring at the sky and their surroundings before looking back to Niði. "Should we try kissing?"

"Th-that depends. What do you mean?" Now he felt like he was shaking like a leaf. There was absolutely no way that Viktor meant what the blond suspected he meant. Still, he *had* to know for sure. He had to hear him say it.

Viktor raised his hand palm up and let it hang between them. He was looking around, up at the sky, off to the left, back to the sky. He was nervous. That made *Niði* nervous. And his hand was just…there. Waiting. He only held his hand up like that when he wanted Niði to hold his hand, but right now, the poor lad was too busy trying to dig his hands into the log. He had to hold onto it or else he might float away and cease to exist.

Eventually, Viktor lowered his hand. Before he withdrew it completely, though, Niði snatched it in his own. He couldn't possibly imagine holding hands with his dearest friend while talking about *kissing*, but he also couldn't bear the regret that he'd feel if he rejected Viktor's offer either.

So silently, they held hands for a moment. And Niði shut his eyes tight, focusing on their hands and nothing else. Even in this moment, it calmed him a little. Only a little. It just felt so natural and familiar, the warmth and coarseness of Viktor's palm against his own. It felt like an anchor.

But Viktor spoke up again, sending Niði's heart skittering. "Should we try kissing each other?"

"Huh?!" Niði's eyes shot open, and he accidentally caught sight of Viktor looming next to him, staring at him. "Wh-what?"

"We don't have to if you don't want to. It doesn't have to mean anything. Just to practice."

"Practice?" Niði squeaked. "Practice?"

But Viktor didn't respond.

The nervous blond couldn't contain his anxieties, nor the fact that his face was burning bright red with flush. Trembling like a leaf, Niði swallowed hard and tried to gather himself up for a response.

Still, Viktor waited. The ball was in Niði's court. "…Okay."

"Okay?"

"We should try."

"Try?"

Niði wanted to scream. Now wasn't the time nor place for Viktor's need for explicit answers, but given that he'd just done the exact same thing to his tall friend, it was only fair and reasonable. They both needed to hear directly from each other's voices. Niði took a deep breath, then muttered, "We should try kissing each other."

Time could have frozen in that moment. Viktor stared at the sky. Niði felt like he might faint. They both had to cope with the can of worms they'd just opened. Much later in life, Viktor confessed to me that he had only suggested the idea of 'practicing' kissing because he sincerely thought that his friend wasn't gay. He'd grown up watching Niði vehemently deny being gay any time anyone so much as considered throwing a slur at him. Viktor, being loyal and trusting of anything Niði ever said, believed him.

Feeling despair at this, he'd hatched a plan, triggered by Luna's pestering, and asked to kiss as a harmless practice run. That way he'd get to kiss the boy he loved at least once. What a sweetheart goofball, right?

Eventually, this would be cleared up for Viktor. Niði was absolutely gay, but he'd built a confusing little complex up about it around himself and struggled to accept it for a while. Thus, the hilariously awkward operation of stealing Niði's first kiss was executed.

Anyway, after a few more moments of silence, Viktor asked, "Is it okay if I kiss you now?"

Niði fought again with his urge to scream. This was very difficult. "Ah, um...Yes..."

And then Viktor kissed him.

Honestly, I couldn't say what happened after that. They kissed and then Niði was much too distracted to focus or think about literally anything else for the rest of the day. The week, the month, the year. The only thing he could remember for a good long while was that first kiss.

The second time Niði ever saw Viktor cry came only a few months or so after the kiss incident. It was autumn by then and for the days leading up to the crying event, Viktor had been nearly mute again. He was withdrawn and thoughtful, not necessarily moody or unkind, but a little lackluster for sure.

Needless to say, his blond friend was worried about him.

But Niði didn't have the courage to ask him anything directly. After all, sometimes Viktor was just quiet and didn't have anything to say, had no reason to emote. Niði worried that maybe there was nothing wrong and Viktor was just having a quiet phase. If Niði had asked what was wrong, he might have seemed like a worrywart. So, regrettably Niði didn't check on Viktor until it was a little out of hand.

The small teen knew he should have said something sooner. When Viktor didn't show up to school one day, Niði's heart sank and his fears were confirmed. Never had Niði known Viktor to miss school. He couldn't even remember a time when the dark-haired boy was ill. So, while reflecting on Viktor's excessive stoicism over the past few days, Niði's imagination ran wild with regret and concern. After school, he decided to go looking for him.

Bolting past Luna, as she stood at the corner, no doubt confused about Viktor's absence, the blond ran all the way to their secret garden. No Viktor. Huffing at this point, he ran to their favorite park bench. No Viktor. The bookstore. No Viktor. The library. No. Nowhere. Where was he?

Out of breath and slick with sweat, Niði scrambled to think of where else his friend could possibly be. He dragged himself back to the forest, clumsily trotting around the winding paths. Scrambling through his brain, he remembered, years ago, when he and Viktor were pretend-playing as vikings, Viktor had taken him deep into a thicket where the stump of a chopped down tree had served as their land-claim.

That's where Niði bolted off to next. Though it took him several more minutes than he would have liked to find it, simply because it had been years since he'd ever thought of the place.

To his relief, that's where he found Viktor, far off any beaten path, hiding behind a wall of thick shrubbery.

"Vi…Vik…!" He panted.

Viktor looked up at him, shocked.

For a long moment, they just stared at each other, taking each other in. Niði, disheveled and sweaty, damp and out of breath, hair clinging to his forehead and cheeks, face burning red from exertion. Viktor, arms unobscured by his usual flannel, bruises bright and glaring, eyes red from crying, slumped posture.

Instantly, Niði flew to him. "Viktor! Viktor! I was looking for you!" Viktor met him halfway and nearly tackled him with a crushing embrace. "I'm sorry," he mumbled. "I'm sorry."

"What happened?"

"I got upset again…I got in a fight with my father. I'm fine now, really…I was just going to come get you," Viktor responded, voice sheepish and still shaky with emotion.

"You're not fine!"

"I'm fine…"

To his credit, the smaller teen managed to break out of Viktor's hold and immediately swung his hand out to gesture at one of Viktor's bruised arms. Viktor looked up at the sky.

"You're not fine, Viktor!"

"It's okay."

"No. It's not."

"I'm…It's always been this way. I'm used to it."

"You shouldn't be."

And somehow, that statement was what changed Viktor's mood entirely. He smiled. Not one of his toothy, blindingly endearing grins, but a soft and gentle thing. He was touched by Niði's adamance.

I'll spare you the details for the conversation that followed. They just sat down together in the grass and shared childhood memories back and forth. Some of them we've already discussed so far. Others, I don't think are super important to the story, but they learned a lot more about each other on this day. They shared their secrets and dreams, confessed their struggles and doubts. Sure, all good things. But they mostly just talked about their favorite memories and spent the afternoon hidden from the world, just like they always did.

O Đ

I don't know if this is the right time to tell you or not, but I think I've finally remembered what my first memory was. It's probably not the most thrilling or most significant thing, but it is something worth recalling. I think. Well, probably not, but it's been on my mind since I started talking to you. So what is my first memory, you may ask?

I remember my mother taking me out to the Christmas Market when I was very young. Three? Four? Five? Somewhere around there.

I had to sing with a group of other children some little song arrangement for the holidays. I remember my polished black shoes, tiny black slacks, and scratchy red sweater that made my neck hot and itchy. I don't remember the song, nor do I remember if we performed it well. Probably not. We were a bunch of toddlers.

Once the song was done, I stepped down from the risers and my mom greeted me from the front row. My dad was holding her hand. I ran up to them and they both hugged me. My father had to go back to work, so he picked me up, gave me a hug, then passed me off to my mother. She was wearing a soft, faux fur purple coat. I liked hiding my face in it because it was so plush and warm.

She carried me out of the little amphitheater and then took me for a walk down the street. The sky was dark and all the little stores were brightly decorated for the season. It wasn't snowing, but it was cold enough outside to believe that it should have been. We walked around the market for a while, and I remember she bought me a hot cocoa and then…that's it.

That's all I remember, but it's pretty substantial, don't you think? That's probably my first real memory.

● A Confession

After completing their mandatory schooling, Viktor got his first job at the bookstore. The one that Erkki owned, of course. This didn't mean he spent much more time with Luna, though he did spend substantially more time with Erkki. Luna was busy with her own life and she didn't have time to bother her favorite stoic friend while her dad was around to, I dunno, bother her in the way that parents so often bother their kids.

Over the course of a few months, Viktor started to recognize the regular customers. Mostly, this included older folks and teens looking for a place to be left alone. Only a few people stood out to him, and one of them was a skittish girl named Halle. She only ever spoke to Viktor if she needed to request help getting something from a high up shelf, but the way she shrank back from him and avoided any other customer stuck with him as something a bit strange. Other notable patrons included an elderly woman with a neck brace, a pallid man who exclusively read only one author's selection of books, and a small kid that liked horses and nothing else.

Viktor continued working at the bookstore for a few years, right up until Niði completed school. Now, I'll spare you the details, but after that initial kiss, the two lads shared a few others, always under some excuse or guise on Viktor's part. In retrospect these excuses were so hilarious and paper thin, that it's almost incredible that neither boy knew that they had crushes on each other. My favorite of Viktor's excuses was this one. "I don't remember what it feels like to kiss, so can I just try again with you?"

One day, after Viktor's shift ended at Erkki's bookshop, Niði met him at the nearby park for a typical afternoon hangout session. He brought two coffees with him, one for Viktor and one for himself, and they sat quietly for the first few minutes enjoying the bitter drinks. This was one of their most practiced routines by this point, so there was little need for pleasantries outside the very nature of enjoying each other's presence.

"I finished that book I was reading last night," Niði eased the conversation to life.

Viktor nodded, absorbing one last second of silence before responding, "How was it?"

"It was nice. Good. Pretty short. I liked it," he said. "It was a bit more of a romantic story than I expected, but I think you should read it sometime too, so I won't spoil it."

Again, Viktor nodded. "Remind me who wrote it?"

"Storm."

"...Huh?" Misunderstanding the response, Viktor tilted his head towards the Western sky.

Niði couldn't help laughing a little at his friend's genuine confusion. "No, I mean, the author goes by Storm. I don't think that's his real name. Or hers? I'm not sure."

Viktor looked back towards Niði and took a sip of coffee. He nodded a third time. "I see," he finally said as he flicked his eyes up and around their surroundings. "What's it about?"

"I'm not sure."

"Didn't you read it?"

"Well, yes, but," Niði chuckled through his response before biting his lip in thought. He gathered his thoughts as neatly as he could before turning his body towards Viktor and rattling off his attempt at the synopsis.

"I think it's about relationships, right? The lives of others and how they all connect. Storm is usually a poet, so even in this book there's a lot of really strange prose. He has a strange way of writing about things, and the story, well, stories, really. They bounce around a lot. It all comes together in the end, though. There's a really emotional part where one of the characters ends up getting hurt protecting someone, right? I totally cried. It was really sweet, you know?"

Seeing Niði so excited about the book brought a gentle smirk to Viktor's face as he watched the blond become more and more animated. After waiting to make sure he'd fully absorbed and parsed through what Niði rambled, Viktor asked, "Did it really make you cry?"

Niði scrunched up his shoulders in a slight shrug and wrapped his hands around the coffee cup in his lap. With a sheepish little laugh, he said, "Yeah. It did. I can't explain it, but it was just so sweet and emotional. They sacrificed themself to protect the one they loved. I'm weak for a good romantic story, though, so it's probably just me being a baby like always."

"No," Viktor said, quieter than usual, "You're not a baby."

The two fell silent for a few beats, left to contemplate their own thoughts and soak in the gentle warmth of the sun. Just when Niði was about to probe his friend for more talk, Viktor spoke.

"I don't think I would sacrifice myself for the one I love. I don't believe in self-sacrifice."

This statement rang out loudly in Niði's head despite Viktor's ever gentle voice. It reached into him and crunched his heart uncomfortably with a whirlwind of emotions and thoughts. The significance of it targeted a sensitive nerve and the implications swirled around Niði's chest like trapped birds in a cage.

"But if anyone hurt you," Viktor continued, "I'd kill them."

Niði's breath caught in his throat and held there until he felt dizzy.

When he started breathing again, Niði hazarded a glance towards his dark-haired friend. Viktor stared directly back at him, intense and tight-jawed. Surprised by the gravity of his expression, the timid blond looked quickly away. He didn't know how to take it, didn't know what to say.

Viktor's proclamation stirred to life a sea of churning emotions against Niði's stomach, the waves of which carried a hopeful longing and giddy relief. In the depths swam a great beast of morbid curiosity, a current of satisfaction in its wake. As the tide of this nervous happiness lapped at his heart, Niði managed to face Viktor again.

"Uh, so, Vik…?" The words begrudgingly came out, slippery and floundering against the tide in his chest.

"Niði. I mean it."

That wasn't the question Niði was going to ask. He already knew that Viktor meant what he said, but his doubling down on the statement kicked Niði's emotions into high tide. It was beginning to feel as though he might drown in those feelings.

The next string of words that poured from him must have come from the deepest trench of that sea. "Is that a promise?"

"Yes."

While Niði's grandmother's health was still ailing, both young men had completed school and there was a little down time before either of them left to pursue higher education. Both of them wanted to pursue their chosen university studies, but they both also had their reasons as to why they hadn't left town yet. Viktor had been tied up by his obligations to his younger brother as well as with his father on his fishing boat. Niði was trying to spend more time with his grandmother while she was still there.

In that time, despite their other responsibilities, the two grew much closer. Eventually, Niði mustered up the courage to tell Viktor how he felt. This happened on a warm summer day as the two sat together in Viktor's room. In all his years of friendship with Viktor prior to this day, the blond had never seen Viktor's home. He understood the whole topic of 'family' to be a bit difficult, so the issue was never pressed despite Niði's burning curiosity. But today was different.

Viktor had the home to himself because his brother and father had taken a trip to Iceland for the weekend. He decided not to go because he didn't want to miss out on a weekend of working at the bookstore. He needed the money. You know how it goes.

After Viktor's morning shift, Niði met him at the little bookshop and Viktor invited him over. He'd invited Niði over with the intent of showing off some of his older, more rare Icelandic books to the blond. Excited for a chance to finally see Viktor's home, Niði happily agreed to go. Once there, they looked at the books for around 5 minutes before Niði made his move.

The blond started this confession with a kiss. This time, *he* initiated it. Of his own volition. Viktor hadn't expected it. They were sitting together on his bed flipping through a book and as Viktor went to reach for another off the shelf, Niði swooped in and planted a peck on his lips.

Viktor froze. He went into computation mode. Niði waited.

Viktor tried to speak. "Ni–"

"I'm gay." Niði confessed.

Silence. Viktor's brow furrowed in thought.

"I never meant to lie to you but…"

Viktor's eyes followed their usual trail, cycled through the up, left, down. He looked at Niði with a curious tilt of his chin. He tried again. "Nið–"

"I didn't know at first and then when I realized it, I was afraid that you'd…I thought you might think I was, I dunno, gross or something. So I lied. I didn't think you'd like me anymore if…If I told you." After he interrupted Viktor for a second time, he sucked in a breath of air and continued, "I thought that I might have been gay before when you smiled at me, way back when I moved here, and then I thought, well maybe I was just confused. My dad says I get confused about a lot of things, and then…And then *you* kissed me and I think I knew then, but I didn't want you to think of me differently so I dunno. I kissed a girl from school once, you know? After you kissed me. I just wanted to make sure, but it didn't feel the same as when you kissed me. I dunno. So, now you know."

Viktor watched Niði and tried to absorb every possible thing he could from his friend. The hunch of his shoulders. The dewy-blue color of his eyes. The exact number of freckles on his face. Viktor wanted to soak in every detail. But as the silence stretched out between them in the wake of Niði's blundering confession, he could tell that Niði was finally done speaking and it was safe for him to try to respond for a third time.

"Niði," he started, hesitating as if anticipating another interruption.

When it didn't come, he looked up at the ceiling and then back to Niði and said, "Did it make you uncomfortable when I kissed you? If I had known, I wouldn't have pressured you into it. I'm sorry." He didn't know how to navigate the conversation and so he gave a messy response without fully knowing if he *should* apologize or not.

"No, no, Vik…" Though he was shivering with nerves, the blond smiled tenderly at his dear, sweet friend, "You never made me do anything I didn't want to do. I could have and *would have* said no if I didn't want it. Don't worry about it. I wanted to, okay? That's my point."

"Okay."

Niði let the silence hang.

Viktor cut it short. "I'm not sure if I'm gay or not. You're the only person I've ever wanted to kiss." With his best friend's sincere confession came one of Viktor's own. It only seemed fair. With that came relief on both ends. He continued, "I like you."

"I like you too, Vik," Niði responded. For so long Niði had worried how Viktor might respond to his admission and how Viktor might feel about having been lied to about it for years before then. Now that everything was out in the open, Niði felt a lot more free. Free enough to laugh. And Viktor smiled as he watched him do so.

"Also, I got a tattoo a few weeks ago. I didn't show you because I wanted it to heal and look good before I showed you," Viktor added with a quick glance at the ceiling.

Niði almost laughed harder. Almost. "Huh? What? Really? What's it of? Where is it?" After having such a tender, nerve-wracking moment, this new bit of news just reminded Niði of how endearing he found Viktor's abrupt topic changes. That and it was truly liberating to know just how much of a non-issue Niði's sexuality was to him. Niði confessed, was accepted, and then they were back to their usual habits.

"Look," Viktor said, proud and pleased as punch. Right before taking off his shirt entirely.

Runes. Elder Futhark. Viktor's favorite. Directly under the left side of his collarbone. All well and good, but the sudden shirtlessness immediately flustered shy Niði. "What, uh. Wh-what do they translate to, Vik?"

After a moment of contemplation, and another glance at the ceiling, Viktor decided not to answer the question. Instead, he drew closer and kissed his friend again. I'm sure you can work out what happened next. I don't need to spell it out for you, but they didn't spend a lot of time talking or reading after that. And Niði never did learn what the runes meant.

O Đ

I bet you're wondering if Viktor and Niði ever got into any arguments, right? That's difficult to answer. I don't think they did. At least not in the way that you might be thinking. They disagreed about a few things, but anytime they did disagree, it almost always came down to misunderstanding. I swear, they didn't really have many fights at all.

I always struggle with arguing and fighting. Conflict. Stuff like that. I really don't like having arguments. I know that they're unavoidable sometimes, but they leave me feeling so drained and empty. Talking things out isn't nearly as bad, but I'm really not fond of fighting.

Unfortunately, there was a time in my life where I was stuck in a constant state of conflict, you know? I wasn't in a good place with my partner and that led to a lot of pain. I know now that I was in an abusive relationship, but sometimes it's tough to see that when you're in it.

Thankfully I can say that there were never such tumultuous times with Viktor and Niði. Maybe that makes their relationship a little boring, but honestly I think it's nice. I am happy that they loved each other and never had to feel much hurt from one another. They already went through enough hurt outside of each other.

○ Intermission

I don't want to spend too much time on this, but a few things happened in Niði's life that ultimately led to him leaving to pursue higher education sooner rather than later. First, his grandmother's passing. This hit him especially hard, though Viktor did his best to be there for him and shoulder some of the burden of his pain. There are just some things in this world that have to be suffered on one's own, however, and mourning the passing of a relative is one of those things. That's not to say he wasn't thankful for Viktor's support. It's likely Niði would have suffered much more were it not for Viktor's attentive presence.

But this was unfortunately not the last of Niði's train of tragic circumstances. Not long after the loss of his grandmother, his parents decided it was time to move back into their hometown. It would have meant that Niði would have gone back North, were he to go with his parents, but rather than do this, the young adult decided that he would finally take the plunge and start the next chapter of his life. University.

Since his beloved Niði was leaving, Viktor had no real reason to linger either. Viktor's brother was old enough to take care of himself, their relationship having stagnated somewhere sour, and his father was still too busy drinking himself into a stupor to care much whether or not Viktor was there. So Viktor decided to leave.

Thus came the difficulty of Niði and Viktor parting from one another. They overcame it by exchanging addresses and cell phone numbers. Niði had chosen to go to university in England. Viktor had chosen to stay closer to home and he would be attending university in Oslo. They both agreed that phone calls would have to be kept to a minimum since it would be expensive to call each other overseas.

Their blossoming relationship had only been defined by blurred ideas and gut feelings. They hadn't called each other anything officially, yet there was this looming sensibility that they were beholden to each other. Viktor staunchly promised that he would always be there for Niði and that he'd always wait for him too, so long as that's what Niði wanted. Likewise, Niði wanted to continue planning for the future, that future being one where they would reconvene and continue into a relationship together. Those were the simple plans and hopes of the two lads. And it was with these hopes that they left for their respective paths.

Unfortunately, this is where everything turned a bit for the worse and a lot of things happened that still pain me to think about to this very day. But I promised to tell their story to you, and I'm here to fulfill that promise. You've been very patient with me so far, and I know it might feel a bit like a cop-out, but I need to do this part quickly. Like ripping off a bandage, you know? This is difficult for me to talk about. I'd much rather go back and talk about their childhood some more but I think we spent enough time there already and I should really get on with it. It's getting a little late, so just bear with me through this arc of the story, okay?

Viktor and Niði wrote each other constantly for the first two years of their university lives. They even made a few trips to meet up with one another when the stars aligned, and those times were as beautiful and magical as your heart could ever imagine. But they couldn't always make time for each other. Thankfully they had grown up knowing what distance and time away from one another felt like, but it was still a little lonely and a little challenging for the two of them.

Every letter sent was a lifeline to each of them. Niði tried to keep every single one. Viktor did the same. They made things work as much as they could have. They made the best of their distance, regardless of the sparse phone calls and the extremely rare visits.

Shortly after completing a term in Oslo, Viktor found that Luna also attended the same school as him. She left for university earlier than he had by a couple of seasons, but the gaps in their schedules often lined up neatly. They spent a lot of time studying together, though since Niði had previously asked Viktor to keep his sexuality a secret, she never learned that the two men had a distinct and dear long-distance relationship with one another. Because of this, her flirting with Viktor became very apparent. Not necessarily to Viktor, as he always struggled a little with reading social cues despite Luna's best efforts. I am happy to report he remained faithful to his childhood crush.

Niði meanwhile did what he could to keep himself busy and distracted. Honestly, being so far away from the only friend he'd ever known was as challenging as it was painful and he really had to focus on everything he possibly could to keep himself from falling into a melancholy. To occupy his time, he set up a few herb planters in his dorm. That and a small handful of newfound friends certainly helped. Apparently, the adult world tended to be a little more accepting of his reserved and demure nature than the children he'd once known.

So the two carried on, working hard for each other. For themselves. All in order to have the future together that they wanted.

And it was good.

And everything was going so well. And then Luna, well. Luna happened.

Luna had always had a thing for Viktor. Now that she didn't perceive Niði as an immediate obstacle, she intended to make her move. This didn't go as she expected.

When Viktor later shared this part of his story with me it was so endearingly *Viktor* that it almost takes the sting out of it. Allegedly, she struggled to figure out how to talk about anything with Viktor that didn't turn into a conversation about Niði. While I do think it's very cute that he was so in love with the lad, I do concede that he probably hurt her feelings quite a bit with his constant fixation. Since she didn't know about their secret relationship, it frustrated her to no end that even without Niði present she still couldn't get Viktor to say more than a few words (unless he talked about Niði).

Regardless of Luna's feelings and attachments, Viktor actually had a lot of trials and tribulations of his own at about this time.

You see, Viktor's brother, Aleksi, started getting into trouble. Serious trouble. Drugs and violent acts of assault kind of trouble. Once Aleksi had gotten a sentence attached to his crimes, Viktor's father finally saw fit to reconnect with his eldest son. Aleksi's first stay in prison was short, thankfully, and Viktor did what he could to try to repair what he could of their relationship when Aleksi got out. Between his father and his brother, Viktor had a lot of emotional hardships to endure.

On top of *that*, Aleksi had had a daughter at some point. This child, with her father fresh out of prison for the first time and her mother nearly absent, needed someone to take care of her. She needed a guardian. And that guardian became Viktor. He did all that he could to bring a sense of normalcy to her life in whatever ways he could.

He tried his best.

Needless to say, this whirlwind of events, from his brother's drug abuse and prison stays to his father's sudden sense of conscience, to a nearly orphaned child, really took a toll on Viktor's mental health. He confided at least this much to Luna.

She was genuinely worried about him. I would have been too. He spent his evenings and weekends driving back and forth from university to home, just trying to help his father wrangle Aleksi, trying to entertain a child, trying to understand why his father had hit him so much growing up, trying to understand anything at all. He was going through a lot, learning a lot, and feeling a lot. He didn't want to worry Niði. Not until he'd worked out his feelings a little better on the whole mess of a situation he'd found himself in.

This is something you already know about Viktor. He really likes to sit and stew on his feelings before opening up about them. He prefers to think through and mull over his responses before opening his mouth. This is just the way he is. So he hadn't immediately confided in Niði for this reason, and I accept that. But it still bothers me a little that he confided in Luna first, anyway.

Regardless, Viktor was tearing himself apart with his family obligations and sense of responsibility, and as a result his grades plummeted. He missed deadlines and skipped classes. He constantly bailed on meeting plans with Luna. She was sincerely worried for him. I really do believe that.

He was seemingly losing himself, feeling pain, having more bouts of silence and mental anguish. At the center of it all, in Luna's opinion, was his insistence that he had to "hold it together for Niði." Those were Viktor's own words. It was a simple sentiment, but this pushed Luna to her limit. She took it upon herself to address Niði for the problem she believed he was causing. She sent Niði her own letter. Without telling Viktor.

The contents of this letter are better left unsaid. Niði doesn't like remembering what the letter said, nor does he even like addressing that there was a letter at all. But there was a letter. The contents of which were enough to crush all of what Niði considered his future certainties.

Because of the cursed thing, the sensitive blond assumed that everything he'd come to share with Viktor had been meaningless. Perhaps it was a little foolish of him to place his faith in the words of Luna rather than the words of his beloved, but such is he.

So Niði slowly retreated. He stopped responding to Viktor's letters and ignored any incoming calls. How could Niði face Viktor knowing that he was a hindrance to his dear friend? He couldn't. He couldn't bear to be the reason for Viktor's struggles. Niði believed Luna was coming from a place of compassion and concern just as much as he believed the haunting voices in his head telling him that he'd been causing Viktor problems for years, and so he shut Viktor out and removed himself from the equation.

Viktor and Niði fell out of contact.

In a cruel twist of fate, after they became unreachable to each other more tragedy befell both of them. Niði's mother passed away due to complications from her illness, and so did Viktor's father due to years of alcohol abuse. Only now they didn't have each other to lean on to get past these tragedies. For the first time in nearly 15 years, they didn't have each other to turn to. Like I said, I don't like talking about this much, so please forgive me for being brief. Just know that when Viktor's father died, it came at a very inopportune time, as usually is the case is with death. But it just so happened to be around when the father and son were rekindling their relationship and so Viktor had exceptional reasons to be sad for it. I feel for him in this way, and I can't imagine how conflicting that felt for him, especially knowing that he went through it alone.

Well not entirely alone, I suppose. He had Luna. She sure made certain that he knew that more than he knew anything else. I think she took advantage of him in his time of need, personally. Especially after driving a rift between him and Niði. This is how she snuck her way into a relationship with him, though it was a rather one-sided affair. I don't know the details of their relationship because I'd rather not know and I've never asked. I do know that he felt at least some affection for her, though. Enough to feel hurt when she eventually betrayed him.

But let's get back to Niði. I still don't want to talk about this, so let's do what we can to get through this fast. When Niði's mother passed, he had no one. This was very difficult for him to manage and process. He took leave from school to mourn and spend a little time with his father. Unlike with Viktor and *his* father, these two had very little to discuss with each other. And when Niði returned to university, he found himself floating in a void of nothingness and loneliness. Until he met Jens.

At the time, this meeting was a blessing to Niði, who had been at a very low point in his life. When the two met, Niði discovered that Jens had come from the same town as his grandmother and that's how they bonded at first. They shared their memories of the town, though Niði left out many of the parts with Viktor. Doing so had made him feel as though his time there had been very shallow and insignificant compared to Jens's. After all, when one person is your whole world for so long, how can you hope to exist outside of that and have the same level of richness as before? Jens and Niði grew closer as Viktor and Luna grew closer, with the chiseled man easing Niði's loneliness, and Luna tending to Viktor's stormy stoicism.

Are you worried about what happens next? I was too. That's why it's so difficult to talk about and I try to rush through it, you know? But I want to tell you the full story, even if it gets difficult.

Sorry. I just needed a break. We can continue now.

● What is Lost

Viktor dropped out of school and moved back home. His father had left him the house after his passing and, since not being in the best mental place to continue his studies, Viktor simply came back home. Luna followed him. I'm not sure if she completed university or not, honestly. I just know that she stayed by Viktor's side for a time.

Niði meanwhile followed through with his degree plan and eventually graduated despite the emotional road bumps. He stayed in England with Jens for a few years after doing so, but was eventually pressured back to Norway at Jens's behest. Niði almost would have rather not gone back, just because, well, there was nothing left for him there. But Jens wanted to go back. Jens always hated England and he made sure that Niði knew that.

Furthermore, Jens wanted to move back, but he didn't want to live together with Niði. He *did* want to keep Niði nearby and continue dating him, but living together wasn't anything Jens had ever been interested in. He said he wanted to take things slow, yet he wanted Niði at his beck and call. I think Jens wanted to have his cake and eat it too.

He needled and needled and needled until Niði caved.

So Jens pushed Niði back to Norway, while Viktor returned with a clingy and equally pushy Luna. That's not to say that Viktor and Niði immediately met up again as soon as Niði was back in Norway. Not at all. In fact, neither was aware that the other was even in that town again for a long while. They'd been out of contact for over five years at that point. Niði probably wouldn't have tried to speak to Viktor again immediately even if he knew they were both back in town, anyway. He would have been much too afraid to meet with him after cutting him off so abruptly.

After a few years of living off of Viktor's charity, Luna had reached her limit with Viktor's oblivious ways. She'd finally gotten what she wanted, but really she hadn't. I can only guess as to how their relationship worked. Knowing Viktor, he probably treated her with his usual stoic respect, but I doubt they crossed into starry-eyed lovers territory. She built the ideal picture of Viktor in her head based on what she thought he was and now he was too depressed and silent to give her what she thought she wanted from him.

The taciturn man was already difficult enough to convince to open up, having only opened up to Niði after years and years of friendship, and he wasn't the type of person to shift so easily towards another person. Coaxing someone like Viktor, even in his best mental health, out of his shell required patience and time. Luna had neither to give.

So she spun around town, found other men to fill her time while relying on the stability of Viktor's home. At first, she kept this promiscuous habit a secret from him. I think she just wanted him to notice her at all, so she acted out. Eventually he *did* notice, and this led to a very long and very exhausting struggle on both ends as neither could figure out what the other wanted. Of course, Viktor valued whatever their relationship had been and so was hurt by her betrayal. She, who had been hurting the entire time they were in a relationship, lashed out at him. They fought in circles until it all came to a head with Aleksi's return from his second stay in prison.

Aleksi's daughter, Lærke, had grown quite fond of her uncle in the time her father was away. She was upset, scared, and sad at first that her dad was gone for a few months, but when he finally returned, she found that she hadn't missed him that much at all. She technically still lived with her mother, but due to the woman's negligence, Viktor ended up taking Lærke for extended sleepovers and little vacations from her home more often than not.

This pissed Aleksi off. So much so that he took it out on the kid. Viktor doesn't like to talk about this much and I don't think he even *can* talk about it without becoming irate. He confided in me about it once years ago, but since he's only told me the story once, I don't know if I can fully explain the course of events here.

What I do know is that Aleksi did something highly irresponsible and there was an ensuing struggle that led to an altercation between him, his girlfriend, and his child. Viktor only caught the tail end of the fight, and it was lucky that he arrived at all, for he'd only stopped in to drop off Lærke's school bag. This event cost Lærke her eye and sent Aleksi right back to prison. Along with his girlfriend.

It scares me so much to think of what could have happened if Viktor hadn't been there. After it happened, Viktor went through every official channel he possibly could to fight for custody and adoption rights of the girl. He succeeded and this is when Luna fully left his side. Viktor wanted to be a parent. He'd always wanted to be one. She did not want to be a parent. She didn't even want to be a faithful girlfriend. So she left him. Then all he had was Lærke, his adopted daughter.

Niði's life, once he'd returned to where it all began, by comparison, wasn't nearly as chaotic. It still wasn't as cozy as he would have hoped, though. For starters, Jens wasn't quite the charming gentleman that he initially seemed to be during those precious first few years of dating. The red flags were there even in England, but they became larger and much more smothering by the time Niði ended up back in Norway.

In hindsight, it was very obvious that Jens cared less about Niði as a person and more about the control he could hold over Niði. Theirs was a difficult relationship to define, but I'll try my best.

Jens worked in law enforcement and as such spent a lot of time away from Niði. He worked long hours. That was fine and nothing to be upset over, but when he was around, Jens was too tired to deal with or listen to Niði or care for his problems. Their relationship became shallow and existed only in brief nighttime visits and snide comments. Jens made the rules, however subtle they were at first. When Niði didn't tread carefully, he'd end up stepping on the landmine that was Jens' spite and anger. Backhanded compliments and harsh jokes became the norm—a far cry from the quiet kindnesses of Niði's previous lover.

Thus Niði had learned to tiptoe over his own feelings, keeping his opinions swallowed before any of Jens's words. He battered himself down into a quiet sort of existence, not fully utilizing his voice or expressing himself in any meaningful way. He felt as though he'd gone back in time decades to where he was a meek little wallflower and was thrown right back into that level of uncertainty. By weathering Jens's insults, Niði made himself small.

Since he wasn't living with Jens, Niði ended up back in his grandmother's house. His father allowed him to live there with a low monthly rent rate. Though living there with all those memories made it difficult for Niði initially, at least he had a space to himself and a place to retreat to when Jens was overwhelmingly difficult to be around.

Niði had even been able to repair and maintain the garden he used to spend time helping his mother grow flowers in. Taking what solace he could in this space, sad to be in as it was, Niði spent time tending the garden and it made him feel vaguely whole again. He recaptured a sliver of his sense of self through his garden and with it felt enough peace to endure everything else. For the most part.

The only thing left to resolve with his move was to find a job. And he found one, purely based on circumstantial luck. He just happened to be in the right place at the right time. Niði had the degree and the abilities, and the school had an opening, so he became a teacher. He taught the lower ages and had a particular focus on science during his lessons. In this way he found numerous small happinesses. Niði was quite fond of his job, in fact. This and his garden were two major players in the game of keeping him sane under Jens's fire.

When Niði first started his job, the other faculty warned him of a girl in his class that had a troubled home life. This reminded him of his dear lost friend Viktor. He wondered if the girl would have similar problems and needs as his friend did, or if he could help her at all in any way. He wouldn't believe any rumors until he met the girl for himself, of course. He'd gone through a lot because of rumors and bullying, so too had his first love, and he'd be damned if he was going to let such a thing happen to someone else in his own classroom. With this strong sense of inspiration and conviction, Niði chased his passion as an educator and prepared to start his next stint in this town as a new man.

Jens scoffed at Niði's determination and told him not to put so much energy into the care of others. He did his best not to let Jens's cynicism drag him down.

O Đ

I bet you can see where this is going, right? Believe me, the threads of events that led our heroes both back here seem entirely too coincidental to be real. Surreal, even. But this is how it happened. Now that we've gotten through one of my least favorite parts of the story, we can get on with the reunion and the bizarre events that followed.

You see, I haven't been entirely honest with you. I was still a little afraid of telling the truth and, to be perfectly clear, some of these memories are a little embarrassing to talk about with you. I don't think I've ever mentioned most of these things to anyone at all yet, so even just talking with you about them has felt a little strange. This has been difficult, to say the least. But I think I'm ready to tell you. I should have introduced myself sooner. My name is Niði.

⦿ How Much Time is Enough?

To say that I was surprised to see Viktor standing outside the school where I now worked would be a gross understatement. I don't know how long I stood there staring out that window, but I remember everything else about the room I was standing in when it happened. The lights were off. I was preparing to lock up the office and go home for the day. All the students were making their ways home too. I had a dark blue satchel with me and it felt so, so heavy. The strap dug into my shoulder. I must have had too many books in it.

And just beyond the glass, standing on the sidewalk was Viktor. It was unmistakably him. He was too far for me to see any finer details, but I knew it was him.

What did I feel? I don't know. Fear? Excitement? Remorse? Longing? Anxiety? Regret? I don't know. I felt everything and nothing. But there he was. *Why was he there?*

Then I saw a young, blonde girl running to him. She was one of my students, only 5 or 6 years old, with messy hair. She ran right into his arms, you see, because he knelt to catch her. A parent and his child.

This struck me as something so painfully rewarding and yet so deeply saddening that I swear I felt as though the ground beneath me fell away. I don't know how I didn't collapse right then and there. Viktor had a daughter. That meant that he'd achieved his dreams, right? Had he found a new 'wife'? He had to have, right? Someone with whom he could have a child with. *Was it Luna?*

All my worst fears, those that I hadn't realized still haunted me, gripped me in place as I watched him turn away (this hurt too), and hand in hand (how long had it been since I'd held his hand?) the two walked to a dull-silver car, got in, and drove away. He must have found new love in Luna, then had a child with her in all those years since I'd last spoken to him.

Even though time had marched ever forward, trampling us in the process, and I should have been content with Jens, it still felt unbelievably, overwhelmingly cheated to see that Viktor had also moved on. That was probably very selfish of me, but the heart is often illogical, and I couldn't explain why I felt the way I did, but that's how I felt so please forgive me for being human and having terrible control over my emotions and wow I really couldn't handle seeing it and I was so upset, I'm sure you're aware, I'm sure you know because I'm so sad even now to think about it and it's all I could do to not fall over right there and I know that you know–

I started to cry.

I had only been teaching my new class for around a week. This small-town school had been a little understaffed for a while, so a very lovely substitute had been filling in for the shortage before my being hired. Now that I was employed, I could rightfully lead the class and free the substitute back to her own devices.

The children were well behaved, creative, loud, fun, curious little things. I've really learned to love working with kids, even if they can be a handful and a little bratty here and there. Of course, I couldn't resist keeping an eye on Viktor's child. She had a bright-purple eyepatch, thick-rimmed glasses, and a constantly messy ponytail. I wondered if she hated brushing her hair as much as young Viktor did. Her name was Lærke and she asked questions about everything, all the time, multiple times.

By the end of the week, I found myself morbidly curious to see if I could peek through the window to see Viktor again, though I admit, even just considering this made my feeble heart start to hammer around my throat. Then a fellow faculty member interrupted my anxiety spiral before I worked myself up too badly to tell me that one of my students' parents needed to speak with me about something. To be honest, it wasn't described very clearly to me and I was still a little distracted by my thoughts. The details weren't that important. It was just that there had been a student that had missed a considerable amount of class very recently and the parent wanted to make sure his child would get caught up on any missed classwork. They wanted to touch base. A reasonable request. So, of course, I put on my cheerful, professional mask and followed the staff member out to the main office to have a chat with this parent.

There he was, looming over everyone else in the room. Viktor.

Seeing him up close was even more heart-wrenching than before. In many ways, he was exactly the same as I'd left him, yet he was much bulkier, a real force to be reckoned with, and his face was a little older, lined with the creases of age. Actually, he had two new piercings. One just below the middle of his lower lip, a stud, and a little nose ring in his left nostril. Viktor with piercings. That made sense to me. He was still wearing black and red and dusty dark jeans, too. He was just the grungy guy I remember. I wonder how I looked to him.

"Niði." He spoke first.

I stood there dumb with stress. I didn't know what to say. I had to stick to professionalism, right? We were at my place of work. I could shove all my personal feelings aside and be the professional I needed to be. I had to.

"You wanted to speak with me?" *Why did I say that?* Such a cold greeting.

"Yes."

The other faculty members must have felt this strange tension between me and this imposing man, just based on the shifting looks and stillness in the room.

"Shall we find somewhere to sit?" *Shall we?* Talking like this was completely unlike me, and yet wearing this strict facade was all that kept me from crippling under the weight of coming face to face with *him*.

"Okay."

I turned and led Viktor towards an open table near the entrance to the faculty offices. It was no bigger than a two-person cafe table and not quite as sturdy or official as a desk. We both sat across from each other, my coworkers now a short distance away. They resumed their tasks quietly once we were settled and I was left virtually alone with Viktor.

When he didn't say anything, I gave him a gentle, verbal nudge. "What did you want to talk to me about?"

Shockingly, he smirked, if only very slightly. "Well…"

My choice of words probably wasn't the best and I should have known that he'd take me very literally. With the grace of a cat on ice, I scrambled to hastily add, "You wanted to talk about your child's progress in class?" Something like that, right? I think that's what my coworker had mentioned.

"Yes, that."

"Okay."

"You weren't her teacher before. I thought her teacher was a woman," he said.

"That was the substitute, they were short on teachers before I was hired."

"I see." The return of the smirk.

And we sat quietly for a few more seconds. I wanted to vanish into my own skin at this point, but obviously that wasn't an option. Thankfully, Viktor spoke of his own volition before I had to again.

"Lærke was absent for three weeks. I wanted to make sure she didn't miss anything important. I just want to keep her caught up and…That's all." Though he concluded himself so simply, I felt like Viktor had more to say than that.

"That's quite a long absence…I can go over what she missed in a few tutoring sessions, if that's the case. I don't think she's missed anything too terribly important, though. I've only had the one class with her, but so far, she still seems to be doing well, so I'm sure we can keep her on track."

He nodded his head, then looked at the ceiling for a moment. I feel as though he looked relieved.

"Can I ask why she was absent for so long?" I probably could have asked my fellow faculty members. I still had a lot to catch up on and learn about both this school and my students, but since Viktor was here, I may as well have asked from the source.

"Yes."

"So, then…Why?"

Viktor shifted in his seat and looked to his left. He looked up at the ceiling tiles, left again to the wall, then back at me. He was uncomfortable, though this was more so apparent in the way he looked around the room, rather than his blank expression. "It's a long story. She…" He struggled internally, battling his words to find the perfect way to tell the story he wanted. Silent for many more moments, Viktor's brow weighed down over his eyes and he seemed to roll his tongue around inside his mouth as he thought. Finally, he leaned closer to me over the table, his already-soft voice diminished into a softer whisper, "There was a…an accident that led to her needing surgery." At this Viktor paused and tapped a finger under his eye. "So she was medically absent."

My mouth dropped into a small 'o' of surprise. "What happened?"

His brow only seemed to furrow deeper. He repeated, "It's a long story."

"Oh…" It was my only response to his way of shutting me out. And that made sense. I had made sure to push him out of my life years ago, so what right did I have to stumble my way back now? Outside of being his daughter's teacher, I probably didn't have any right to know anything about Viktor or his life anymore.

He stood up.

Slowly, so did I.

The conversation was over, as far as Viktor was concerned. He'd gotten what he needed from me, and that was that. Check in about his child's progress, then go. Transaction complete. And yet, it made me feel so empty. What did Viktor feel about seeing me again after all this time? Was he struggling at all? For the first time in my entire time knowing him, I felt like I was back in that first summer with him. I couldn't tell what he was thinking or feeling with the same level of ease as I once could. Not anymore.

Silently, we trudged back to the entrance. It felt like a funeral procession to me. I walked with him all the way outside, though I couldn't fully explain why. I just did.

A short distance from the school entrance, he stopped. I nearly collided with his massive frame.

"Niði."

"Yes?"

"I'll tell you what happened next time."

I nearly leaped out of my skin. *Next time.* The word tumbled out before I'd realized. "When?"

Viktor's back was still to me, but I'm almost certain he was smirking. Something about his response just *sounded* like a smirk. "Who knows? Tomorrow? This weekend? You can just meet me at Erkki's bookshop. I'll tell you then."

Right. Viktor was the patient sort of guy that had always just waited for me to show up. This was usually how our plans worked out. He was *always* waiting for me. Now we had a newly agreed upon place. It was up to me to pick the time. Part of me wished he'd grown out of this phase, and just made plans like a normal adult, exchanged phone numbers perhaps, but this was just Viktor's way. It was as maddening as it was endearing.

"Okay," I said.

The first time I made my way to the bookshop, Viktor wasn't there. But Erkki was, and he greeted me like an old friend. Just like Viktor, Erkki had seemingly barely changed at all, save for gaining a few more wrinkles and pounds as well as losing a bit more of his silver hair. But he was the same kindhearted booklover that I'd befriended as a teen.

He gave me a better timetable for when to expect Viktor to be around. It seemed that because of his new full-time parent status, Viktor had gotten a job at a local hardware store. He worked roughly the same hours as his daughter's school-time so that he could have his evenings and weekends free to be with her. A friend he'd made that owned the local cafe (who in Erkki's words was a charming young lass) sometimes helped babysit Lærke. She even went so far as stealing the girl away for a 'girls only' slumber party here and there. Her name was Malika, Erkki told me, and she was around my age.

If she'd managed to convince Viktor to let her have Lærke for the evening, then Viktor would usually come to the bookstore to occupy his free time.

So that was more or less the newly updated schedule I had for him.

With this information, I was able to find him on my third try. The third time's the charm, I suppose.

When I walked into the shop for this third time and saw Viktor sitting there, I felt both relieved and nervous. I had never felt this way about seeing him before. Had so much time apart made me start to be afraid of him? Was I just afraid because I felt guilty for cutting him off? I didn't want to think about it for too long.

I sat down across from him without a word. Coincidentally, he'd sat at the same table we'd always sat at when we were younger.

He looked up from a thick, yellowed book and smiled slightly.

"Hi, Viktor."

"You want to hear the story now?" Always straight to the point. He never gave a preamble to anything.

"I do." I did.

Viktor dove right into it, after a deep breath and a glance around the room. His face was dark and all curled with saddened eyes and a heavy glare. This wasn't a story he took any joy in telling and, as I've mentioned before, I don't really like this part either. He told me about Lærke by starting with Aleksi.

"Aleksi had a daughter with some woman. She was worse than my father's ex…"

I nodded quietly.

He continued, "She left Aleksi alone a lot with Lærke. Turns out, he's a shit parent, too." Viktor paused and took another breath. He looked at the ceiling, looked to his left, then spoke a little softer as he said, "Aleksi acted a bit like our father did, but…he also did a lot of drugs on top of drinking…He was abusive and he did a lot of things that I think I'd like to punch him in the throat for. We tried to get him help, but…"

I watched Viktor as he spoke and I saw from his tired gaze that this was difficult for him to talk about. Every time he paused to think through his next sentence, I found myself wondering if he would continue. Thankfully, he did. "Well, he never sticks to any of the programs and just falls right back into substance abuse…My father and I tried to help him and Lærke a lot but after he passed–"

"Aleksi died?!" I blurted out.

"No, our father. Sorry…That was unclear of me."

"Y-your father?!"

"Yes."

"I'm…I'm so sorry, Vik," I was stunned. What else had happened since we last spoke? Instinctively I reached across that table and put my hand on his arm. He uncrossed his arms and lifted his hand towards me. I panicked and pulled back. So he held still. I know what you're thinking. I wasn't afraid of holding Viktor's hand. I know he would have tried to take my hand right there because it was as comforting an action to him as it was to me, but you know. I was afraid of Jens. I couldn't be seen holding another man's hand. Especially not Viktor's hand. Do you understand?

I still saw the way Viktor's eyes flicked up at the ceiling at my nervous rejection. I saw him struggle with himself internally. He reviewed my reaction and seemed to guess (correctly) that I was avoiding holding his hand. So he chose to continue his story instead.

"I don't know exactly how it happened…but his stupid fucking girlfriend was arguing with Aleksi and it turned physical. Somehow… Lærke got caught in the middle and…" Viktor hesitated, and I saw his face go pale, his jaw tight. "She fell on broken glass and her eye…I took her to the hospital."

"You were there?!"

"No. Not at first. I had just taken her back home, and I noticed she had forgotten her school bag in my car. I went back to bring it to her. I don't know how everything got out of control so quickly, but…I took her to the hospital and she needed surgery. That's why she was absent for so long from school," Viktor concluded with a sigh. The more he told of the story, the more the rest of him tensed, until he was white-knuckled and grim of expression.

"I'm glad that you were there, Viktor," I offered, meek.

"Yeah," he said. "Me too."

"So…What happened with Aleksi?"

"He is in prison, and I've adopted Lærke."

Short answers again, he must be tired of talking about it. I understand, it must have been a bad experience.

"Adopted?"

"She is my daughter now."

Though it shouldn't have, knowing that Viktor merely adopted his brother's kid rather than having a child with Luna made my heart skitter around my rib cage. Looking back, I think this feeling was hope. This feeling was immediately replaced with guilt as Jens's face loomed in my mind. I was, after all, in a long-term, committed relationship with another man at this point. I shouldn't have been falling in love all over again with my childhood crush.

Though, with the way things were, it was much easier to fall in love with Viktor again than it was to remain in love with Jens.

But, anyway.

Viktor and I talked for a bit longer after that, mostly just about Lærke and her schooling. He had a few questions about children overall and it was really sweet to see him taking on the role of the parent so wholeheartedly. I know that it meant a lot to him and I was happy to help. It was clear that despite wanting to be a father more than anything and finally having a chance to step up to that responsibility, he was very out of his depth.

He knew logical and pragmatic duties. He knew how to take care of another human at a base level, but he didn't quite know how to raise a daughter and all the pitfalls therein. Neither did I, honestly. I knew how to teach and I knew how to talk to children, but I think a lot of these burning questions of Viktor's just had to be learned through experience and time.

⊙ NI(Ð)I

One of my other favorite memories of Viktor was from when we were talking about our favorite Norse gods. I might have mentioned it before, but I've always been fond of Freyja. I liked that she was so beautiful and yet still such a strong figure. I think that's what captivated me the most about her, even as a child. And she had a chariot that was pulled along by cats, which is probably the coolest sort of chariot animal I can think of.

Anyway, I told Viktor about my love of Freyja many times, and I eventually even asked him what his favorite god was. He thought about it, took his time as usual, then told me he really liked Óðr. When I asked him why, he told me that Óðr was Freyja's husband. Yes, before you ask, this was after the legendary 'wife' conversation. Years after, in fact.

I didn't know what he meant by that then. I was still in the closet and a little bit dense and a little too afraid to hope that Viktor might share my feelings. So of course I laughed, and said this was a silly reason to have a favorite god. But then he said something that I still think about constantly.

He said that Óðr was mysterious and little was found to be written of him, and what some scholars believe is that he was Freyja's husband indeed, but that he had to leave her for periods of time. Freyja was known to cry for her husband as she waited for him and the dwarves coveted these tears as a most beautiful treasure. What he said next was that Óðr might have left, but he was certain that the god must have longed to return to his wife more than anything and surely he would return and find her again no matter what.

I told him it was sort of a sad but sweet story. Viktor had only made that stupid beautiful grin in response and he left it at that.

◉ Indecency and Tirelessness

For the next few months after my reunion with Viktor, everything went smoothly in my life. If we ignore the usual arguments with Jens, at least—which, I tried to. Viktor and I continued to meet up in the bookshop to chat at least once a week. Erkki sometimes joined us with coffee and book recommendations. Lærke, too. Sometimes Viktor brought her so that they could read and study together, and that was always a lovely sight.

But the atmosphere was shifting. There was something weird taking place. One of my colleagues, the sports teacher, an entirely average, athletic man named Jonas was making numerous attempts to get close to me.

At first, I thought he was just being friendly and extending his companionship to me as I was still considered the 'new guy'. But he stood far too close to me when we spoke and the way he licked his lips between each sentence gave me the impression of a hunter imagining the flavor of his prey. Does that sound strange to you?

Maybe you've never had the displeasure of being hit on by a creep at a bar, or you've never had to tell a person 'no' that didn't want to take it for an answer, but they all share this uncomfortable presence. It's not something wholly tangible, and I can only speak from my gut instincts, but let's just agree to say that Jonas gave me bad vibes and that if someone gives you that feeling, you should probably avoid them.

It was initially harmless, of course, and I assumed it was just a classic case of personality differences. I was fine with that. We would never be the best of friends because he creeped me out too much, but he was a kind fellow and treated everyone around him with respect. So I did what I could to try not to let my judgments get in the way of our professional relationship.

But he really wasn't respectful of my boundaries. Not really. And this part of the story is difficult to tell, too.

I know you probably remember that I was never fond of any sort of gym class or sports events. We had to swim sometimes in school, and those days were always the worst because we had to be shirtless. I just didn't have the confidence to expose my slim frame to a bunch of jocks and goons. I sincerely understand the feeling of disliking physical exertion, especially as a quiet little bookish kid.

So when I discovered that little Lærke had taken to dodging those classes, I tried my best to empathize. She was a sweet child, having just recently had her seventh birthday, and she was usually very bright and engaging in class.

She completely shut down when I gently tried to urge her to go to swimming class. This was very unusual for her.

Despite my best efforts, Lærke simply refused to go to any of her sports classes and that was becoming a little bit frustrating for me. Not that I was frustrated at her, of course. I wanted to help resolve the problem, but over the course of a week, it seemed more and more like I was going to have to involve her father, Viktor, in the problem-solving of this situation.

Jonas even tried to help me as I attempted to get her to go to class. This was reasonable enough, because he was the head instructor for most of our school's sports. He was the coach. He was the teacher. He was the guy to ask for all things physical education. I thought nothing of it when he offered his assistance.

There I was, talking it over with him, expressing my concern for Lærke and her needs, when he put his hand on my shoulder. He had already been standing too close for comfort, as was his usual habit, but this was a bit much for me. I retreated back a step, trying to put some distance between us, but his grip on my shoulder was firm.

"Now, now, Niði," he said, licking his lips again. They must have been so chapped by then. That's sincerely what I thought in that moment. He continued, "Don't you worry about Lærke. I'm sure we'll figure out a way to get her to rejoin class. You just leave it to me."

Something about the way he said it disturbed me. But the way he held my shoulder bothered me more in the moment and that was my immediate problem so I pulled away and probably found some hasty excuse for ending the conversation. I couldn't stand being near him anymore, so I left.

It was either that day or the next that I went back to Erkki's shop. Viktor wasn't there. I don't think I expected him to be there. I just needed to be surrounded by something comfortable and familiar.

Before you say it, no, absolutely not Jens. He was never really that interested in cuddling or providing emotional comfort. He told me that I was ugly when I cried and the sound of my sniffling annoyed him, so I just went to the bookstore because it made more sense than trying to force my partner to console me. There was a guy there. Maybe a teen, even. I couldn't guess his age. Young adult, probably.

He was chatting with Erkki, so I went to my usual table and sat down. I tried to do so quietly and attract as little attention as possible, but the pleasant old man greeted me anyway.

"Hey, there kiddo," he said. Even though I was already 30 at this point my older friend still called me 'kiddo'. I liked it. "You're lookin' a bit deflated. What ails you on this beautiful day?"

"Oh, just…You know. Trying to think of how to help one of my students." I didn't want to give too much away. Erkki knew both Viktor and his daughter, so I didn't want to breach any privacy unless Viktor was present and gave consent. Also, I hadn't even told *Viktor* about my worries regarding Lærke yet, and he really should be the first to know.

"That's mighty good of you. I'm sure you'll work it out. You're a reasonable lad." He had such a casual aura of kindness. I was quite fond of Erkki. Viktor was too.

The other man spoke up, too. "Oh, you're a teacher? What do you teach?"

"I teach the younger age groups, so I'm a bit of a jack of all subjects, you know?" A nice, easy response.

"I see, I see. I grew up here, but I don't recognize you. Oh! I mean, you're probably too young to have been one of my teachers, though…" He rambled in a way that reminded me of myself. "So, what's your favorite thing to teach?"

"I like to teach about Earth sciences the most. And a little about zoology and such."

"Ooh, that's really rad. So, is one of your students falling behind or something?" He looped it back around to my own silly comment.

As I tried to think of another way of dodging the question and preserving Lærke's privacy, who do you think finally showed up?

The soft creak of the door announced his arrival, and with a small wave in Erkki's direction, Viktor paced right up to the table I was seated at and looked me over.

"Hi, Viktor."

"Hey, cool teacher guy, do you know if that sports coach is still there? Mr, uhh...Jonsson, Jonas?" the younger guy called out to me with a different question.

Viktor scanned the three of us silently. I wished he would have just sat down already.

"Y-yes?" I answered the question with a little confusion.

"Man," the guy said. "You know he's a drug dealer, right? Kind of a weirdo, too. I always hated him. Gosh, I'm surprised nobody's told on him yet. Oh well."

"Huh?" Why was he telling me this? I melted a little into my chair.

Erkki saved me from having to respond in full, though. "Is that so? Can't say I've met him." With a thoughtful whistle, Erkki gazed out at the three of us and shrugged. "I thought I knew just about everyone in town, but my guess is that he's not much of a reader, else I woulda met him by now."

Viktor still hadn't sat down. Instead, he was watching the younger man with a blank expression. I knew he was thinking through something. I could practically hear the gears clicking through his thoughts, but I couldn't tell *what* he was thinking. I could just tell that he was thinking very hard about *something*.

"Niði." I hadn't expected him to speak since he was so deep in thought, and I nearly jumped out of my chair. "I'm going for a walk. Come with me."

You know, I realized what Viktor was doing then and relief flooded my system. He was giving me an escape in the only way he knew how. Seeing my discomfort, Viktor decided it was time for me to leave and thus he asked me to come with him so that I could have an elegant excuse. Just as he'd always done. My heart ached with this realization and I nearly stumbled all over myself to get up and follow after him as he turned and walked out of the store. I think I heard Erkki chuckling, but it could just as easily have been the sound of the door creaking as it swung shut.

Viktor took me to our park bench. A perfectly reasonable, perfectly public spot for two life-long friends to be seen together. You may already have assumed, but I felt a little nervous about being alone with him, just because I knew Jens wouldn't approve at all.

Oh? Have I not mentioned that yet? Jens was absolutely *not* a fan of Viktor's, but I'll tell you about that in a minute. Let's get through this part of the story first, before I forget.

Viktor looked at me. I looked at him.

"Is Lærke doing okay at home…?" I started. This was probably as good a time as I would ever have to start this conversation.

He looked at the sky. I watched his eyes slide across the landscape in his ritual thinking pattern. "She's quieter."

"I see. But she hasn't said anything strange to you, right?" Viktor took a deep breath. I braced myself.

He said, "I don't know."

"What…What makes you uncertain?"

"Well," he closed his eyes and deliberated a bit before continuing. "She says she doesn't like doing sports. She doesn't like swimming. I've asked if she's afraid of water or…if she just doesn't like exercise. She shakes her head and won't tell me more. I don't know what it means."

I said this with my gut instinct and, to this day, I'm not completely sure if I really had the justification to do so. What I said caused a chain reaction of events, you see. While in the end my gut instinct turned out to be correct, it was still something a little careless of me to have said, and, well, the memory of this moment sometimes haunts me a little. But I said it. If I couldn't confide in Viktor, then who did I have? Please don't say Jens. We'll get to that, though, I won't forget.

"I…Viktor, there's someone…"

"Someone?" His eyes narrowed and I watched his face flatten even further into an extremely tense blandness.

"There's this instructor. His name is Jonas Jonsson, we were just talking about him at the shop, actually, and he—"

"He what?"

For once, Viktor was quick to jump in and interrupt me. Though his voice was soft and level, he was angry. I could feel it. I knew it wasn't directed at me, but the sheer force of his fatherly protectiveness was a little crushing. A little strong and unbearable.

"I think he's the reason Lærke is hiding from class. He makes me uncomfortable too, and just now, that guy in the store…Well he thinks Jonas is suspicious too and…And he grabbed my shoulder—"

"He touched you?" I felt like all of Viktor's attention had been sharpened to a point and stabbed into my chest. Why was this so difficult to express and did he know just how difficult he was making it to speak?

"W-well, it wasn't as if he hurt me, but...Yeah. He makes me uncomfortable, and that young man in the store just now—"

"Halle?" Viktor snapped.

"Halle...?" I echoed.

"Fuck. That...was his name. Nevermind. Someone I know."

"Oh, ah, well...Anyway, Halle said that that teacher deals drugs and, and, and, I dunno it's just weird and I don't like it! I don't know, Viktor, but I don't like it. He makes me feel so uncomfortable and I'm worried about Lærke!" I just blurted it all out without taking a breath.

Viktor lifted his hand, then promptly set it back down on the bench. I wondered what he wanted to do. Did he want to hold my hand? Again, I kept thinking about his hands and how long it had been since the last time he'd taken mine and led me somewhere. I had followed him all the way here, of course, so in a way, it was almost how we used to be. I missed those days though. I missed Viktor. I missed holding hands and talking to him. More than anything. I think I even started to cry again.

Except, this time, I couldn't lean on him. He was right there, right next to me, and I couldn't touch him because *what would Jens do if he saw*? I just needed a friend to comfort me. It wasn't even anything to do with how much I still loved Viktor, but it was just a stressful day. I was afraid for one of my students, my best friend's daughter, and I just wanted someone, *anyone* to be there with me.

Viktor was there, but he sensed my reservations and respected them. He didn't move an inch towards or away from me. But because he was respecting my space, that only made me want to cling to him more. I couldn't. I just couldn't. Not with Jens in my life.

I guess we should just talk about Jens now. The conversation between Viktor and I ended around then, anyway. He walked me back to the bookstore and we discussed snippets of things. I think he was trying to distract me, but the damage was already done. So we just talked about the trees, the different stores we passed and what they'd once been. Light, soft memories.

After a short time, I went home. Jens wasn't there. He was working. Not that he often paid me any visits, anyway. Usually, I just went to his apartment whenever he had time for me. I had convinced myself that this was just how our relationship should be.

Anyway, let's get this out of the way.

○ Jens

Jens grew up in the same town as the one Viktor had moved to as a child. They lived on opposite sides of town from one another, with Viktor living in a pretty remote farmstead at the very edge of town and Jens living closer to the main streets, within walking distance of most modern amenities. He was around Viktor's age, too. Maybe a little older, but it couldn't have been by more than a year or two.

They'd had very few run-ins with each other as children, though they got into at least a few scuffles. Usually during the school year, and usually only when one or the other was provoked. Being provoked for Viktor meant being called 'trashy' or 'rabid'. Being provoked for Jens meant anyone looking in his direction while also being Viktor.

Jens saw the weird Viktor as nothing more than a sloppy, freakish, stupid kid and he hated him from the moment he laid eyes on him. They were basically like water and oil to each other. But, for the most part, they didn't really run into each other much, thanks to being in different grades and living in opposite directions.

Jens also had a particular posse of friends that he tried to keep himself surrounded with and Viktor was too busy hiding in the forest or helping out his father to really see any of them. Jens never met Niði in his youth, though that wasn't too surprising. Niði wasn't there for much of those childhood years and Jens moved to Bergen with his parents sometime in his teen years.

Jens never viewed Bergen as his home, though, so he made up his mind to move back to his hometown after completing university. This is why he'd been so adamant with me about it after we'd met and started dating. I guess he'd just been home sick.

I've already talked about the part where he and I met and bonded, thus starting our relationship and this and that, so I won't go over it again. I will say that those first few months together were really charming, but fairly surface level as far as casual dating goes.

Jens was a charismatic man, had soft, sandy hair, cropped short, and easy green eyes. He was muscular and polite. Not too distinct, nor too bland. I found him handsome enough. Plus, he had aspirations to work in a police department, and was keen on someday working towards a law degree. He might have wanted to be a lawyer, but when I met him, he was content with staying firmly within the boundaries of law enforcement.

Though Jens had no interest in literature (or reading of any kind), we had similar interests in nature. He and I took a lot of hikes together over the initial few years. He was never really interested in *learning* about any of the natural wonders that we explored, but at least we had that one hobby together. Sometimes, I even convinced him to go to various museums with me. I'm just trying to say that we had a few things that we could share together despite our relative indifference towards each other's interests otherwise.

But the more I got to know him, the more I noticed that we had a lot of contrasting ideas as to what our relationship would be going forward. This was a big source of conflict initially. Jens wasn't keen on the idea of starting any sort of family, which was something I at least wanted to remain open to. He wasn't really that interested in displays of physical affection, either. I was the type of person that liked physical touch and comfort. He wasn't much of a kisser, and this may be too much information for you, but intercourse was always just a means to an end. This made me feel a little neglected, here and there, but I made the best of things.

Steadily, our relationship stagnated and got worse. Jens was very hardheaded and stubborn. He didn't like to be wrong, nor did he like to be corrected. And at first, I don't think I had too much of a problem with this, but then he started to get a little more spiteful with each debate we had. I think he took every suggestion, every conversation, every comment, as a personal attack. So he attacked right back. I'm sure you can relate. You know what it's like to argue with your partner. Did you ever say anything out of anger and not mean it? That happens from time to time with couples in moments of high stress.

But I think Jens always said exactly what he meant, even in those moments. I just didn't want to believe that he meant it. I wanted to believe that he'd merely spoken out of anger rather than anything else, but that's not true. I know that now. I knew it then.

Thankfully, he never got extremely physical during our spats. He'd pushed me before, that's true, and he slapped me whenever I seriously upset him, but he never punched me or anything, so I weathered it. Besides, he'd always come around and apologize eventually, in his own way. If I was sure to give him space and not talk back, everything would settle down and Jens would be okay again. We only ever argued whenever I made mistakes, too, so once I'd learned to avoid making those mistakes, we fought less. I learned how to tread lightly.

There were a lot of times when I wished I was more like Viktor. I wished that I had the strength to fight back. Jens deserved to be knocked down—at least a few pegs, you know? If only I was strong or brave enough… It was a lot to endure, and some days were worse than others, but thanks to years of experience, I was an expert at enduring.

What else should I tell you about Jens? To be honest, he's not in my life anymore so I try not to think about him. I mostly feel disgusted when I think about him now, knowing that I had tried so hard to salvage a relationship that was more pain than happiness. It sort of hurts to think about him.

Jens frequently told me to stay away from Viktor, as I briefly mentioned before. You know, when he learned that Viktor's daughter was in my class, he told me not to have anything to do with the kid. Told me that there was nothing good that I could teach a kid from *that* family. He even went on to slander Aleksi a little for the drug abuse. I don't think he knew about the whole adoption situation, but he knew (as did the whole town, apparently) about Aleksi's addiction struggles.

I don't think Jens ever knew about just how close Viktor and I had been as children because I avoided talking about him with Jens as much as possible. Sure, Jens knew that Viktor had been a friend of mine, but I danced around the depths of our friendship. There was already enough bad blood between the two of them, so why add more fuel to that fire? Initially, I had never told Jens about him because the pain was still too fresh for me. When we met, I was still in mourning—both the loss of my mother and the loss of contact with Viktor.

But telling him didn't matter so much, because Jens was always at work or 'too tired' to talk to me most of the time. He was always too busy to spend a night with me. We saw each other less and less throughout our relationship, yet I still felt bound and committed to him. I sincerely believed that Jens would spend more time with me when he had more, well, more time to spend. So I endured the neglect and bitter comments just because that's what a good partner would do. That's what I told myself.

I chose this relationship, after all. I pushed Viktor out of my life and welcomed Jens in. While I do think that part of our relationship boiled down to a sort of self-punishment on my part, I also sincerely clung to all the false hope my heart could manage. Hindsight revealed many ugly truths to me in this way, despite how backwards my logic may have been at the time. As miserable as I was with Jens, I thought I deserved it.

And that's all I want to say about him for now. I hope that cleared up enough for you, because there's not much else I can say.

⊙ I Don't Read Newspapers Often

I was on the bus one morning making my usual commute to work, and I caught sight of a suspicious headline on a nearby passenger's newspaper. I was so shocked when I saw it, that I nearly spilled my coffee all over the gentleman who'd been reading said paper. Clumsily, I fumbled with the napkin in my pocket and hastily wiped the mess I had made off of myself and the seat between us. The man gave me a grumbling huff before turning back to his paper and I remained stunned well into my workday.

Local Resident, Jonas Jonsson Found Dead in Church

Dead? *Dead?* How? Why? When? Viktor?

A billion thoughts warred for attention in my scattered brain but all I could cling to with any sort of coherence was *thank goodness*. Which, for all intents and purposes, is quite a cynical thing to think. But more than anything, I wanted to know in my gut if this had something to do with Viktor.

It had been two weeks since I'd confided in him what I'd felt, and I didn't really think much of it after, but now that conversation burned fresh in my mind.

I'd told Viktor about my fears. Now a man was dead.

But hey, that didn't mean anything. Right? It could have been a coincidence. The headline said 'dead', not 'murdered'. And yet, I couldn't shake the nauseous feeling that there was so much more to this story than I could possibly imagine. Dead, dead, dead. Jonas Jonsson found dead.

No more creepy vibes. He was dead.

There was too much on my mind. When I got home from work that day, after teaching and hiding my feelings behind the joys and delights of being around children, I called Jens.

"What?" he answered.

"Did you hear about the, the uh…"

"I don't have time for this. The what?"

I swallowed and took a deep breath to still my thoughts, then tried again. "Did you hear about the death?"

"The murder, you mean?"

"*Murder?*"

"That fucking weird-ass coach from your school, right?"

"R-right…So, it's a murder?"

"Yeah. Listen, I'm busy right now."

"Oh," I said, my stomach dropping through the floor, my head floating above the clouds in a dizzying buzz. "Yeah, sure. Sorry about that. I'll see you later?"

"Maybe. Bye."

I wanted to say 'bye' back, but he'd already hung up. Jens wasn't a detective or anything, but being in law enforcement, I'm sure he had his hands full with *the murder*.

I still couldn't stop thinking about Viktor. I had to find him. I had to know what had happened. I needed to talk to someone. He'd picked up Lærke from school as he always did. I think. I saw his car, at least. But where had he gone after? Would he be at the bookstore? Would he be with his daughter? I shouldn't talk about murder in front of one of my students, right?

But I had to find Viktor. I had to see him.

Still standing in the foyer of my home, I looked down at the flimsy little phone in my hand. Viktor had given me his phone number years and years ago and I wondered if it was still the same. I hadn't called him in over five years.

My hands shook as I dialed Viktor's number. As I held the phone up to my ear, sweating, dizzy, and anxious, I struggled with my thoughts.

"Niði," he answered, voice soft as ever. "Are you alright?"

I laughed some strangled sound. Relief, comfort? Was I alright? I certainly hadn't expected him to answer, and I definitely hadn't expected him to ask me *that*.

There was a long pause. I was catching my breath from what I realize now was a panic attack and Viktor was sitting there on the other end of the line listening to me. Eventually, he asked again.

"Are you alright, Niði?"

"No, not really. Viktor, d-did you know…?"

Silence. Then, "I can come get you. Where are you?"

"Did you know that the sports instructor was murdered?" I practically hissed at him.

"Yes. I saw it in the newspaper."

This stilled the franticly flapping thoughts a little. He'd seen it in the newspaper. That made sense. It made me feel a little bit more grounded in reality to hear him say so.

"H-he was murdered…" I was still a little too out of sorts to form any coherent thoughts, so I uttered this with a weak wheeze.

"Where are you Niði?" Viktor sounded calm. He was always cool and collected, completely unlike me. I began to feel a little silly for being so overwhelmed by the news. Maybe I had been jumping to conclusions.

"I'm at home." I answered.

"Do you need me to come stay with you? Are you alright where you are?"

"I'm fine, I'm fine Viktor," I don't know why I lied. I should have told him to come over then and there. His kindness was more than I deserved in the moment, having only thought of him as a potential murder suspect for the whole day. I started feeling so foolish and guilty that I almost broke into tears, but I managed to hold them back.

"Are you sure?" He was giving me one last chance.

"I'm sure." And I squandered it.

"Do you need me to stay on the phone with you?"

"No. I'm sorry, I just…" I couldn't be honest with him moments prior, and yet here I went, blurting out my feelings as soon as they slammed into my head. "I just wanted to hear your voice."

Dead silence met me, and I swear I could almost picture his blank expression, the one I was certain was on his face. It was such a Viktor-like response that I laughed again. I didn't know what to say, so I just laughed.

He chuckled a little too and, I wondered instinctively if I'd ever get to see his wide grin again.

"Thanks, Vik. I think I'm okay now…"

"Okay."

"Well, then–"

"Niði," he interrupted.

"Yeah?"

"I'm here if you need me. You can call me any time, okay?"

Always so direct and kind, Viktor was. I should have called him much, much sooner. I had missed this feeling and I felt more than a little guilty that it warmed me so much to hear him say that.

"I know. Thank you, I'll…I'll call you if I need you."

"Okay."

And then we said our goodbyes.

It was rare that Jens would agree to a dinner outing with me, but after reading about my colleague being murdered, I just really needed some comfort. I called Jens again after getting off the phone with Viktor and begged for him to come see me. I know that it was selfish of me to do so. I know Jens was already stressed with work. I know. I just needed to see him.

Despite his moodiness and resistance to the idea, Jens finally caved and agreed to the date. So I did what many people often do and made sure to dress nicely for the occasion.

Jens came over to my home with the intent of walking to the restaurant together. He waited on the sofa in a surly silence and picked at a loose string hanging off of his sweater, waiting for me to hurry up and get ready. It didn't take me long, but it was still enough time to turn Jens' mood for the petty.

Still, I wanted to try to make the evening a pleasant one, so I ignored the passive-aggressive sighs and eye-rolls. I didn't even flinch when he said, "I don't know why you bother. You look the same as always."

The walk to the restaurant was mercifully uneventful and quiet. As I mentioned, Jens wasn't one for physical affection, so there was no handholding of any sort, nor any playful touches. Anyone who saw us would just assume this was a friendly outing and nothing more. That's how Jens preferred it.

Since I still had my own reservations against being perceived as overtly gay in public, I had no problem respecting Jens' wishes. Though I did wish that Jens might have been just a little bit less cold and sterile that night, for even close friends often smile and touch each other in some capacity.

That was just how it was with Jens at this point in our relationship.

Once we got to our destination and were shown to the table, we sat across from each other. Jens immediately burrowed himself into the menu. I passively watched him from the edge of my vision and tried to focus on my own menu perusal. Of course, I didn't want to be rude and try to talk while he weighed his choices, so I stayed quiet up until the waiter approached.

After our orders were placed, I found it a suitable time to attempt conversation. "How was your day?"

Jens gave me a look-over with an expression that seemed to convey that he thought I'd grown another head. He said, "I'm tired. I worked all day, dealt with idiots nonstop, and now I'm here."

"I'm sorry," I responded with a nervous exhale. "I hope this helps, at least."

"What?"

"Dinner."

Jens scoffed a bitter little chuckle in response. I should have known that this was going to be an uphill struggle.

I pressed a sympathetic smile onto my face and buried any tension as far down as I could manage. Jens was in a bad mood. That was obvious. But I did sincerely want to make it better. Maybe I could bridge the gap between us by sympathizing. So I said, "I didn't have the best day, either."

Jens bared an indifferent glare.

"It's nice to see you, though. We haven't done this in a while," I said, trying a different tactic.

"Yeah." The response was very impassive.

After sitting in awkward, sullen silence for far too long, I made a final attempt at breathing life into the conversation. I was determined to turn the mood around and have a pleasant dinner with Jens. Despite it all, I truly thought that such a thing was still possible. "I met with an old friend the other day."

Jens glowered in my direction. The coldness with which he regarded me made me regret even bringing it up.

I pressed on regardless. "We met at that bookshop. The one just down the road, you know?"

"Who was it?"

"Oh, just," I hesitated, the stern stare of Jens's intense gaze causing me to falter. "My old friend, Viktor."

"You mean your ex?" I should have lied and said Erkki's name instead. I shouldn't have mentioned Viktor. To this day, I'm not even sure why I mentioned Viktor to Jens. Maybe I actually did want to argue, for once. Maybe I wanted to instigate and lash out.

"No. We never dated. He was just a friend," I responded quickly. A half-lie.

Jens was just as unconvinced with the answer as I was. "Bullshit."

I tried to smile earnestly, but the damage was done.

"That's the fucking guy you used cry about all the time," Jens accused.

"Well, yeah. He was my best friend! When we lost contact, it was hard on me. But that's all, really." I kept piling on those half-lies. Or half-truths. Either way. I always hated confrontation and arguments, but part of me also found it cathartic. If I was always waiting to step on a landmine, I was often too stressed to enjoy myself in any capacity, but if the mine was already triggered, it was easier to let it all out. Does that make sense?

Anyway, with an incredulous laugh, Jens leaned back against his chair. He jabbed a finger at me and said, "Weren't you the one that told me you couldn't talk to him anymore because you cut him off?"

"Well, yes," I responded, caught in the half-truth.

"So then, why the fuck are you talking to him again?"

Here was a question that I could answer easily, innocently, and truthfully. "His daughter is one of my students."

"So what? Isn't he gay?" I didn't expect him to ask me this in response, but I think I knew what he was getting at and all my guilt resurfaced before I could clamp it all back down.

"I don't know about that," I mumbled sheepishly. "But I told you his kid was in my class already. That's how we got in contact again."

"So, now you're prancing around town with him like old times, huh?"

"No," I insisted with a boldness that I didn't know I was capable of. The catharsis won over the anxiety. "Well, I do plan on seeing him again at the bookstore, but that's hardly a crime, is it?"

Jens's fist colliding with the table seemingly silenced the entire restaurant. I immediately wished I could take back my idiotic quip.

"Don't fuck with me."

"I'm sorry, Jens. I'm not trying to argue." I was well past the point of half-lies and half-truths by this point.

We stared at each other for an uncomfortable amount of time. My power of will crumpled as I fidgeted in my seat nervously.

"Next time, why don't you just invite him to dinner."

"No! What?"

Then Jens stood and left. I didn't dare go after him and I didn't hear from him again for a while.

Like I mentioned, the town was abuzz with gossip for a few weeks, but I paid it little mind. There was a mild stir once the news came out that Mr. Jonas Jonsson had been quite the purveyor of pornographic material, most of which too disgusting for me to want to bring up. The folks who'd clutched at their chests and previously bemoaned fears of safety suddenly found themselves besmirching the dead man instead.

I didn't want to hear about any of it anymore and I rather wanted to focus on my students and quietly mind my garden instead, return to normalcy, if possible.

That said, I spent the night with Jens for the first time in three weeks. This gave me little, if any, comfort. Though we did share a relatively peaceful dinner together, neither of us were in the mood for chatting. When we went to bed, he turned away from me and when I woke up in the morning, he had already left for work. There was nothing violent or explosive about this night, but the hollowness that I felt after spending it with Jens stung all the same.

I found myself falling further and further into an inescapable hole that I was digging entirely myself.

I called Viktor again. I called him more and more frequently, every time I couldn't find him at the bookstore. Soon enough, we were on daily speaking terms again. If we didn't see each other in person, one of us would call the other. It felt just like it had years before and we talked about anything and everything. Except for Jens.

I had my best friend back and all my students were thriving and happy, including Lærke. My workplace was no longer stressful to be in. Everything felt right. Well, almost everything. I was still beholden to a shitty boyfriend, but I didn't feel that bad that I didn't spend time with Jens as often.

A week or two passed, and I found myself dreading when I'd see him next. He never really saw fit to call me, so it really had been a while since he and I had last spoken. He must have been really busy. Or tired. Or both. Maybe he finally forgot about me. Maybe I was free.

Jens did call me eventually. He wanted to come visit me in my home. Spend some time together. It might disappoint you to hear this, but I asked him what he wanted me to cook for dinner, asked what time he'd show up, and the plan was made.

Jens's visit was more of a curse than a blessing, as his hair-trigger temper was exceptionally thin this time, and I'd earned his wrath by not having purchased the proper ingredients for dinner. So a full-on arsenal of insults were thrown my way, along with a particularly fragile glass full of water. It was a whole shouting match with one participant. It was better to weather these mood swings quietly, lest they spiral into the exceptionally spiteful commentary or more than one broken dish. Needless to say, I was nauseous with stress and fear for the remainder of the night afterwards and well into the next day as well. Unbearably so. I was hitting my limit. Though I had brought this all on myself, it was becoming clear that something needed to change.

He slept in my bed that night. He lounged around on my couch all morning. I decided to take a book and go for a walk and put some space between us. This wasn't without resistance, but ultimately, Jens let me leave the house with only a little arguing.

It was very likely that if I stayed out long enough, Jens would either go to work or go home by the time I got back. So I wandered for a good long while before finding a place for myself to settle and unwind. The sky was a little grey, but the weather was moderate, and before I knew it, I'd found a lovely little corner of the park that I hadn't noticed before and tucked myself into a bench.

It would be dishonest of me to say I hadn't called Viktor nearly as soon as I'd left the house with the intent of meeting him at this particular spot, but it had been a spur of the moment thing. Honest. I had been lucky that he wasn't busy spending time with his daughter and had caught him during his downtime. He had been in the area already, actually, since he'd just dropped off Lærke with Malika for the afternoon.

It took him a few minutes to find where I'd parked myself, but he found me soon enough. It looked like he had a book in his hand, too. How silly it was that we had changed so much and yet so little as we grew up. I found it charming that we were both still so taken with the idea of strolling with books as our only companions. Nothing had changed in that regard.

Viktor sat next to me, set the book in his lap, and let his thumb idly flick up and down the worn, feathered edges of the pages. With a brief inhale, Viktor looked up and around a few times. He was considering his words, as he always did, and eventually he said, "It might rain today. Are you planning on staying outside for long?"

"Oh, no, not particularly," I responded, looking at the sky for myself. The clouds didn't look too particularly heavy, so I'm not sure if he was speaking with internal conviction or if he'd seen the weather report. "I just needed to be out of the house for a bit, you know? I was feeling a little stir-crazy. Are you staying out for long?"

With a pause to consider his answer, Viktor leaned his head back and closed his eyes. It must have been an interesting question, because it took a little longer for him to answer than usual.

"I'll probably stay out to feel the rain for a bit. Then I'll go home." He couldn't possibly give an actually quantifiable answer, but he gave the best answer he could, regardless. I watched him as he sucked in his lower lip with thought.

"It might be a while before I go back home, but I'm not sure. Lærke is staying with Malika for the night and I have a lot of free time right now, so here I am," he concluded with a shrug.

"What did you bring to read?" I asked, pointing to the book sandwiched between his hands. "Want to read it to me?" With a hopeful expression and a tilted little smile, I tried to stare at him with what I thought was a very convincing expression.

To my credit, Viktor responded with a small huff of amusement. "You want me to read this to you?" He lifted the book in one hand and hit me with a smug smirk. "I could do that. But would you believe what I read to you? Do you trust me?"

I knew this game and I was willing to play. I just had to let him know. "Of course I trust you, Viktor."

"Oh?" and then he leaned much closer to me than I'd expected him to and I realized that I'd made a severe miscalculation. He opened the book, glanced at it with little attentiveness, almost as if he was only looking for the show of it, then he whispered in my ear, and I can't bring myself to repeat to you what he said.

Anyway, I blushed and nearly fell off the bench in my flustered surprise as I jerked back away from him. Thankfully, Viktor leaned away to laugh and though he'd earned a loud *"Viktor!"* from me, I joined him in laughing. I could feel my post-Jens-argument anxiety melting away with each breath.

"You don't believe me? You don't think that's what the book really says?" he teased, the half-moon curl of his lips quickly approaching a dangerous territory.

"No! Absolutely not! That's *not* what that book is about!" I argued between my laughter. I should have known that this would happen.

Very rarely did Viktor ever take any of my requests for reading out loud seriously.

"You never know…" He hummed with a warm smile. When I gave him one final, playful shove, his body didn't budge an inch.

Then he finally beamed at me for the first time in years.

Viktor grinned at me and I was lost all over again with all my feelings. That stupid grin. His stupid crooked tooth. His stupid eyes. His stupid everything. And me, stupid Niði, who had given him up and pushed him away years ago. I let it go and now I wanted it all back. I was selfish. I wanted Viktor back. I was so fed up with the arguing and neglect with Jens, that I couldn't help myself.

Without thinking, and with a critically low level of braincells, I kissed him.

And for a very, very, painfully long, heavy, stupid, long, long, long amount of time, neither of us did or said anything. I planted my mouth against his for an inordinate amount of time, and then couldn't bring myself to pull away. We just froze together for a moment.

He told me later in life that he'd been so surprised at me for doing that, that he didn't know if he was even allowed to kiss me back or move. Because I didn't move, neither did he.

Well okay, eventually I did move. I panicked and pulled away from him and apologized profusely. And then, before he did anything, he asked me, "What are you apologizing for?"

And I said, "Ah, um…Because I kissed you?"

And Viktor laughed. He said, "Never apologize for that." And I kissed him again.

And he kissed me back.

And that's how I started cheating on Jens.

I'm not proud to admit it, and you may sympathize with me, here, but that's what it was. I was cheating on my boyfriend. I was having an affair, emotionally and physically. It was a long time coming, but I just couldn't hold back anymore, not with Viktor.

I don't know how you feel about infidelity or things like that, so you may think that sharing a little peck in the park is hardly anything to write home about when it comes to cheating on one's partner. But over time, we did more than that. I'm a little embarrassed to admit it. Try not to judge me too harshly, but don't take what I did as something excusable either.

It only started with those two little kisses in the park. Sooner than I could have predicted, we were meeting in his house, sometimes even at my house, sharing private moments together that culminated into more things than they probably should have. At the time, I excused it all away because, well. Because. Because I hated being with Jens. I hated him, too. I hated Jens, okay?

I hated the way Jens made me struggle for every ounce of kindness. I hated the way he pushed me away and pulled me back in on a whim. I hated how every time he smiled at me, I felt slivers of hope, stabbing me in the back every time he yelled. Being with Jens felt like being caught in a tornado. It was unbearable. Every time he went a week or longer without contacting me, I hoped and hoped and hoped that he was finally done with me and that he'd never come back. And I hated myself for running back to him every time he did eventually come back.

I hated that Jens didn't like learning new things. I hated that he never read. I hated that he drank beer every time we were together and I hated that he always made me cook. I hated his disdain for others and the rude way he talked about everyone. I hated the way he shoved me and the way he called me names. Most of all, I hated that Jens wasn't Viktor.

As frustrating as it is to admit, the more time I spent with Viktor, the more I realized how unhappy I was. The more evenings I spent with Jens, the more it started to weigh me down. Being near him as he ignored me to watch television, having my every movement and every word criticized, even just being in the same room as him in passing. I could hardly even breathe around him without worrying if I was going to set him off in some way.

I took walks a lot more frequently.

On one of these walks, I just happened to see something that made my heart freeze into place. I held my breath and felt my heart start to pound. Everything went numb.

Viktor was walking with Luna. *Luna.*

I liked her about as little as I liked Jens at this point, for different reasons, of course. Though I don't know if my dislike of her is a fair assessment for me to make, really. I just held a lot of things against her, like losing years of time with Viktor, ending up with Jens…I blamed her for a lot of things then, though I know now that probably isn't the most fair thing for me to have done. Still, she did play a large part in driving me to push myself away from Viktor and as it was, I blamed her for a lot of my unhappiness.

Needless to say, seeing her with Viktor was a lot for me to take in.

I don't know why I did it, but I slipped off the side of the path and ducked behind a shrub. Classy, I know, but I didn't want to be discovered by her at that moment. I wasn't quite ready to face her with all the other things going on in my life at the time and I don't think I could handle it if I made Viktor worry about me. So I hid behind the plant like a literal cartoon character and peered through the leaves to watch them as they passed.

As she articulated her complaints with much gesticulation, Luna's exasperated tone carried a certain whine to it that grated on me. "I just don't see why you think it's such a bad idea, Vik."

"I don't care." He cut her off. It felt a little satisfying to hear him do that.

"But it worked out for the better, didn't it? I can help you. I *can* be better. If you hadn't ignored me, I wouldn't—"

"That's not my problem. I don't care." He didn't give her a chance to finish her thought.

What were they talking about?

"Is it because I'm not ready to be a parent? God damnit, Viktor! You made the decision to adopt her, not me!" Luna was nearly shouting and her gestures were becoming a bit more frantic.

"Exactly. So, leave me alone."

"Once Aleksi returns from prison, what are you going to do?"

"None of your business."

"And Niði—"

"Don't!" As Viktor cut her off and halted in his tracks, I saw something I had never seen him do before nor have I seen him do since. He shouted. "Don't you dare!"

Luna was probably just as surprised as I was, just in the way she flinched at the sound. From my vantage point, her back was to me and he was facing her. Viktor's broad frame vastly overshadowed her petite one. As uncanny as it was to see his calm expression as his voice boomed, I found myself to be quite the fascinated observer. I was a morbid voyeur, taking part in a scene that felt dangerously personal. Yet she'd said my name.

"Why is it always about Niði?!" I was impressed to hear Luna yell right back. "When will you notice what *I'm* going through?"

For the first time in a very long time I felt a pang of sympathy for her. I wanted to see from her perspective. I wanted to believe she was a good person. I really, really did.

Viktor didn't respond to her.

"You have a problem. You're obsessed," she accused flatly.

"No, *you're* obsessed! No normal person would keep…doing this! After being told I'm not interested! After everything you've done!" His head ducked down as he yelled, as if the sound of his own voice was too much. I couldn't see his eyes clearly, but in his silent pause, I knew he must have been looking around. "Why won't you just stop? Why did you *have* to interfere?"

She'd struck a nerve with that comment. I'd never heard him take this tone before, and it was a little difficult to listen to. "Stop it, Viktor. You're…You're hurting yourself." I leaned further against the leaves as she said this and struggled to see what she saw.

From this distance, it was difficult to tell for sure what he had done, but by the way she took his hands and smoothed them between her own, I guessed that he'd clenched his fists so tightly that his nails must have cut into his palms. I'm still not sure to this day, but that's my best guess. They lowered their voices much more after this point and continued walking.

I couldn't hear anything else they were saying. Whatever they were talking about, Viktor wasn't happy about it. I admit, this made me feel a little happy in a way, since the idea of Luna taking a casual stroll with my dark-haired Viktor and them being super friendly didn't exactly spark a lot of confidence in my feeble heart. Yet seeing him so upset didn't sit well with me. I was relieved in many ways that their stroll hadn't been one of friendliness, but it made my head spin knowing how hurt he'd been because of it.

I wanted to know what they were talking about and what it had to do with me.

So, I asked Viktor the next time I saw him, a few days later. It was during one of our more discrete meetings, if you know what I mean. He had come over to my house after Jens had left town for the weekend to visit his family in Bergen.

As I sat next to Viktor hand in hand on the couch, he told me that he'd seen me behind the bush as he was on his walk with Luna. Immediately, my face reddened and warmed with shame. I'd been found out. Had Luna seen me? Gods, I hope not.

Viktor simply explained to me their conversation and revealed then that after he and I had lost contact, Luna and him had been in a very brief and un-happy relationship together wherein she cheated on him and ultimately told him not to adopt Lærke. He didn't give me too many details and only really delivered the direct facts, but the death of his father and the subsequent struggle to adopt Lærke had been the straw that broke the back of their relationship entirely on her end. Nothing was going to keep Viktor from loving and protecting this child, and that bothered Luna greatly. Apparently, she started cheating on him in an effort to grab his attention. Or so she told him. I thought it sounded like a pretty weak excuse.

He told me that when I'd been "hiding behind the bush like a loon", Luna had been trying to get him to be in a relationship with her again. He'd told her no and that he had no feelings for her anymore, as a friend or otherwise. So she kept following him and bothering him and this and that, thus the minor spat I witnessed.

I asked him what she meant when she said my name. He said he didn't know. He didn't want to hear what she had to say.

Though it did feel good to hear that he had no feelings for her whatsoever and that he had no intention of letting her weasel back into his life, knowing that she was around at all still filled me with a sense of dread. Viktor must have known this, because he gave me a long stare and said, "Don't worry, my dearest *Freyja*, I'm not going anywhere."

I'm extremely unhappy to report that a short few weeks later, Luna contacted me and asked to meet me for lunch. I went because of course I did. You might think I'm a bit stupid for doing so, but that's just the kind of person I am. I may have held a lot of contempt in my heart for her and I may not like her much as a person, but after seeing her argue with Viktor, I guess I just I wanted to give her the benefit of the doubt. Or maybe I just wanted to know what she had to say about me. Probably a little bit of both.

So I went to meet her at a local cafe. Malika's cafe, in fact. Though Malika herself wasn't working that day, apparently. On the walk there, I felt increasingly trepidatious. Sure, I was a little curious to see what Luna had to say to me after all this time, but I was beginning to realize just how much I didn't actually want to see her. Every step brought me that much closer to her and I could feel the tension in my chest tightening down on me like a vice.

I regretted entering the building even before stepping foot in it.

Once I sat down across from Luna, I was painfully reminded of just how striking she was. I hadn't seen her clearly during her argument, but her eyes were as round and as they were glossy, her hair long as it was sleek. Her face was distinctly foxlike and beautiful, as it had always been. For a split second, the vice on my chest pinched down in an ache of envy. I hated that someone so underhanded could be so beautiful.

"Hiya, Niði," she started, as if we'd remained close friends.

Nervously, I took in my surroundings, finding it difficult to look her directly in the eye. The table was a lovely dark wood with a lacquered finish, the paneling on the walls painted a gentle grey lavender. Malika had good taste in interior design, that was for sure. Oh, but I still had to respond to Luna.

"Hi. It's been a while," I said.

She smiled. "Yeah, it really has. Have you been doing well?"

"I don't mean to be rude, but why did you want to meet with me today?"

Despite seeing her from a distance somewhat recently, coming face to face with her after all this time, while a little less emotional than my reunion with Viktor, crushed my chest in anxious tightness. The contents of her letter blared in my ears as if she herself had spoken them to me rather than written them.

Viktor is suffering because of you. He can't stand having to take care of you and his family and school and himself all at once. You should stop trying to pressure him with your weird clinginess so much because watching him fall apart over you is sickening.

"Fair enough. I'll get to the point, then," she hummed, not at all bothered by my directness. I don't know why, but this irked me. "I think you should stop playing your little games with Viktor."

The whole room suddenly felt as tight as my chest and it became increasingly more difficult to breathe. I asked, "What do you mean?"

She answered, "You know *exactly* what I mean."

"I don't." But actually, I think I did.

"Oh, really? Didn't you invite him over to your house the other day?"

I probably looked like an unraveling mess and I could feel my stomach being shoved up into my throat by the hammering of my heart. I was insulted by her insinuations, no matter how correct they were.

Of course I invited Viktor over to my house. It was *my* house. I could invite over whoever I wanted. Why did everyone always care so much about my personal affairs, anyway? Why did everyone always treat me this way? From my father to this 'friend', as far back as I can remember. I was always everyone's doormat. I was sick of it. So, so sick of it.

With a dry mouth and significantly tighter throat, I responded, "We've been friends for years, Luna. You, me, and Viktor. Are you saying I shouldn't be allowed to invite friends over to *my* house? Isn't that something friends can do?"

"Sure, sure. But is sucking each other's dicks something friends do, too?" Unbothered. Obnoxiously pretty. Her not-so-subtle accusation hit me like a freight train.

I was so nauseous and dizzy, I felt as if my head had swollen to be the size of the room. I couldn't feel my body through the dense claws of an oncoming panic attack, but I still managed to push myself away from the table and stand up.

"Wh-what are you saying?"

"Cut the shit, Niði."

"You cut the shit!"

"I'm not the one fucking around."

"Viktor is…He's just my friend!" Luna smirked, those foxlike features suddenly wolfish.

"Friends? You're nothing but the clingy faggot boy that won't fuck off already." I hated that she looked so smug; always acting like she was better than me. "Satisfied now that you've finally trapped him again?"

"Trapped? No, he…" I felt like I might faint. Or cry, if I wasn't already doing so. Viktor and I always clung to each other. He always took *my* hand, after all. "We care about each other…We're best friends. What are you talking about?"

I was thrown right back into those preteen years, face to face with another tormentor. "You *know* what I'm talking about."

My brain leaped and bounded across lanes of logic. The cheating I understand being called out for, but not the rest. Through my hurt and rage, I couldn't process anything.

Not my thoughts.

Not what Luna was saying.

Not what color the floor was.

Though I was staring at it through a thick veil of tears.

All my memories of Viktor and our conversations rolled around in the undercurrent of my cascading thoughts.

"I thought you'd stopped bothering us years ago. I thought we had an understanding, Niði," Luna practically purred. How could she do this to me so publicly and calmly? I wondered if she'd always been like this and I simply didn't notice.

I fumbled for a response, but none came.

With blurred vision, my eyes darted around at the other patrons. Our spectacle was being politely ignored.

"Why do you keep coming back?" she continued. "Why couldn't you just stay away and let him go? I wanted to be with him too, you know? And you always got in the way." Steadily, Luna's voice rose from her usual volume until it pierced my ears. She was too loud. "Even when you weren't there, you were in my way."

"What are you talking about?" I found my voice long enough to hiss, "What does *this* have to do with *that*?" I didn't want to talk about my adultery. I obscured it through vagueness and cowardice, unwilling to confess it out loud.

"So you're admitting it, then? That you've been *fucking* Viktor?" She said what I didn't have the courage to say. I didn't have the courage to deny it, either.

She was right.

No matter how much I wanted to scream in her face—no matter how much I wanted to slap her—I was still the weak coward I'd always been. Enduring was my strong suit. Self-defense was not. How I wished I could have had the courage then and there to do anything to stand up for myself.

I'd walked right into a trap by coming here and there was no good way to escape. Yet, out of the corner of my eye, I saw the door to the cafe open, and in walked the young man from the bookstore. Halle? I thought that was his name. That's what Viktor had said, I think.

It was the only lifeline I had at the time and I was sinking fast.

"H-Halle?" I called out, no doubt in the most strangled sounding voice possible.

The man looked at me with a quizzical expression, and looked torn between answering me and ignoring me, so I tried again.

"Halle, it-it's been so long since I've seen you." I was already walking towards him, face full of tears and a weak sense of reality in tow.

Much to my relief, he decided to go along with my weird act. Luna glared at me from her seat at the table but didn't get up to chase me or yell at me or anything. This buzzed a strange little laugh out of me, because she'd never gotten up to follow me and Viktor when we left, either.

Not once.

I don't think I was in the right headspace to reminisce, though, so the thought train ended there as I made eye contact with the young man.

To his credit, Halle managed a fairly genuine looking smile and reached out to clasp his arm around my shoulders. I managed not to flinch from the surprise of it, and with that he said, "Hey there, friend. I thought that was you! Saw you from the window, thought I'd peek in and see for sure. How have you been? You're lookin' a little rough. Let's get some air."

With his grip on my shoulder, he turned me around and guided me out of the cafe. I didn't dare look back. I probably would have collapsed if I had.

Outside, Halle let go of me. Not immediately, but quickly enough for me to feel a little embarrassed. We walked in silence for a few paces until he finally said, "My name is Sindre, by the way."

"Oh, gosh…I'm so sorry…"

"No, it's fine." He waved a hand dismissively and shrugged. "I used to go by Halle. Did Vik tell you that was my name?"

"H-huh? You mean Viktor?" It shouldn't have been super surprising in a small town, but it was definitely strange to hear someone use Viktor's nickname so casually by someone Niði assumed was just an acquaintance.

Sindre smiled at me a little sadly. He gave me a friendly nudge with his shoulder and said, "The very same. When he met me a few years ago, my name *was* Halle. I just wasn't sure if he'd told you that or not. But, uh, listen. So, what was going on back there? You looked like you were in a bit of trouble."

My face, already hot and red from crying, burned even hotter from the shame and embarrassment that threatened to crush my chest. I owed Sindre both an explanation and gratitude for letting me use him so abruptly to escape. I took a deep breath, let out a long sigh, and tried my best.

"Yeah, I wasn't doing so well…I sort of walked into that one, but it… Anyway, thank you." I struggled to even provide a minor explanation. Where should I even start? And with a stranger no less?

"Hey, Niði, right?"

I nodded, sniffling and pawing at my face in a fruitless endeavor to wipe the tears.

Sindre put his arm around me again and gave me what I'm sure he meant to be a reassuring squeeze. "I kind of know a bit about you, actually. I'm sort of a friend of Vik's, yeah? And he's told me about you plenty of times, so—"

"*Sort of* a friend?" I interrupted.

He nodded, but kept talking on his original trajectory, "I think I already know what this is about. More or less. You don't have to explain yourself, and no worries about uh…No worries about dragging me away from the blessed promise of coffee, huh? Want to go sit somewhere or, uh, something? Need anything?"

I was a little too outside myself to fully appreciate Sindre's offer just yet. I was pretty hung up on what he said initially, though, so I asked again, "You're *sort of* a friend of Viktor's?"

"Yeeeeaaahh…I mean, I'm *pretty sure* we're friends. He's my friend, so I'm probably his friend," he said in a singsongy voice as he gave a little shrug. "Sometimes, I help him around the house, or I watch over Lærke for him. I've picked her up from school a few times, but I was using his car, so you might not have noticed that it was me and not him."

The significance of Viktor trusting this man with Lærke's wellbeing was not lost on me. And if dark-haired, awkward, protective Viktor trusted this young man, so did I. At least enough for the time being.

You know what else? I did vaguely know of Sindre's existence, I just hadn't pieced together that it was him that was spoken of before. The more the fellow rambled, the more I somewhat recalled Viktor mentioning him in the past. As both Halle and Sindre. Here and there, this and that. I'd heard of him, for certain. I just hadn't yet realized that I had.

"Oh, well…Nice to meet you, Sindre."

Sindre laughed a small, sultry little sound, something like a very cultivated and practiced chuckle that was put on for show more than for actual amusement. It wasn't an unkind sound, though. "Nice to meet you, too, Niði. Happy to meet you officially for real and stuff."

"Likewise." I think I was calm enough by then to be left alone. We'd walked a little ways together and my home wasn't too far from where we were. Maybe a five-minute walk away. Ten, tops. "And thank you for helping me. I appreciate it. I'm just going to go home, now."

"Need help getting there? I can at least walk you there, if you need."

"No, thanks. I think I want to be by myself for a bit."

"Groovy. I get it. Well, take it easy. I'm going to go find, uh, probably somewhere else to grab a coffee, then. But, anyway, catch you around!" And with that Sindre released me, spun on his heel, and sauntered off in the opposite direction.

As promised, I walked home. In a hell of a daze, I didn't even know what parts of the day failed to register. I was again upset about the letter situation and hurt by her (correct) accusations of my cheating. I shouldn't have gone to speak with her. I really, really shouldn't have, and I'd learn that much more painfully than I'd already thought I had by that evening.

○ NI(Đ)I

Maybe it's a little morbid, but sometimes I wonder what my last memory will be. I think the most boring answer is that your last memory would obviously be whatever is happening at the moment of your death. And sure, I think I understand that reasoning. Some would even go so far as saying that everything we experience is a memory, even the very instant you're experiencing it. So are you ever living in the present? Is everything already a memory?

Maybe this is getting a little too abstract.

Anyway, sometimes I wonder what my last memory might be and why it might be whatever it is. Would my last memory be of Viktor? Would I think about my father and the strained relationship we had? Would I think of my mother and her softness? Or maybe my grandmother and her warnings of trolls and elves. If I had to choose a last memory to go out on, I think I'd like to make it a really good one.

Viktor actually met my parents once. And my grandmother. It was when I finished mandatory schooling and he'd come to my house to bring me a celebratory gift. The gift was small, and he'd been able to hide it from my father because of this. He'd made it just for me though, and he slipped it into my hand as carefully and sneakily as he thought he could.

It was a little grass ring, woven tightly around some thread. There was a little bundle of purple flowers tightly pinched together like a miniature bouquet in place of a gem. Instead of yet another crown, he'd given me a ring. I put it in my pocket as carefully as possible.

My grandma, who was sitting on the porch, asked me to introduce her to my friend and I, being an obedient boy who adored her, did just that. As Viktor stood in front of her, crooked smirk, black leather jacket, torn up dark denim jeans and all, he looked so much larger than her. She was a petite lady to begin with, but she looked so tiny compared to him, even buried under her throne of quilts and pillows.

My mother came out to see what the commotion was, then I had to introduce her to Viktor too. Of course she had a lot to say about what a strapping young lad he was. Then my father came out and stood to the side of my mother. They both smiled politely and asked Viktor a few questions about himself. He answered a little bashfully, but navigated through the conversation quite well, despite his nervous glances at the sky and at the shrubs to the left of him.

My mother, being a sentimental kind of person, demanded that I stand with Viktor to take a picture with him. So we stood in front of the garden, with all the beautiful flowers sprawling out behind us, and my mother held up the camera.

At the last second Viktor threw his arms around me and squeezed me with his big dumb grin on his face. The shutter clicked. The flash flared in front of my eyes. He released me and laughed heartily. My mom laughed too, told me I had a really good friend in him. Years and years later, Viktor told me that before he was allowed to leave with me, she had pulled him aside and told him to "take good care" of me and winked. I had to run inside to grab my jacket, so I hadn't seen this take place, but it just adds another layer of warmth to the memory for me.

And before you ask, yes. I still have the little purple flower ring. It was one of the few gifts I was able to keep with me throughout the years.

All of my family and every person I had ever loved in one spot. That's the memory I'd like to leave this world with. That's the thing I want to have on my mind before I go.

◉ What is Beyond a Silver Lining?

Jens came over to my home early in the evening of the day I had my 'chat' with Luna. He didn't call ahead of time, which wasn't entirely unheard of, but it still struck me as a little odd. He was so cerily calm as I asked him how his day was and what he wanted me to cook for dinner that I immediately felt something was wrong. Everything felt wrong. Even the air felt wrong. If you've ever been in a relationship like mine, then you know what I mean.

You can just tell when something is about to blow up. You know, I thought for sure that I was going to come clean that night about Viktor. About my feelings for him. And my (very different) feelings for Jens. but I hesitated and became too afraid to speak because of this distinct and uncomfortable atmosphere.

I felt it in the way he looked at me. I felt the wrongness in the sneer of his lips and the smug drowsiness in his eyes. I knew that tonight was going to be bad. I just had no way of knowing just how bad it was going to be.

I'll spare us both the gory details, because I'm afraid I won't be able to finish the story if I go too much into it. I just have to say it.

Jens seriously beat me for the first time that night.

And then he drank himself into a stupor as I cooked him dinner. As it turned out, he overheard me and Luna earlier. He was there all along in the booth behind us, waiting and listening, all at her request. My mind raced along and I thought of just how much I hated both of them. Him and Luna. I hated them both so much, I thought I would burst. I hated them, I hated them, I hated them.

And I was so, so tired of being treated this way. Something had to change. Something had to be done. *I* had to do something. Anything.

As I finished preparing the food, Jens tried to shove me again, tried to attack me with one of the beer bottles that shattered on the floor, but thanks to his inebriation, he was a little too clumsy, and I was able to lock myself in the bathroom during the assault.

I was terrified, honestly.

I thought he was going to knock down the bathroom door at first with all his pounding, but I think he passed out at some point, because eventually he stopped screaming and slamming everything.

Thankfully, I had my cell phone stashed away in my pocket, so as I sat there, crying at the base of the toilet, I called Viktor.

"Niði." I don't know why he always greeted me this way, answered the phone this way, with my name. Every time. It was one of his many consistencies and one of the many reasons I loved him. I loved him and hated Jens.

It took me so many tries before I could speak. I don't even know if I actually did speak. I couldn't stop sobbing and I feel like any time I opened my mouth, my throat just whined like a creaky door. If I said any coherent words to him, I'm not sure what they were.

"Where are you?"

There was an urgency to his voice that was enough to make me start to feel safe again. Not enough to speak coherently, but enough to start breathing again.

"I'm coming."

He must've known I was at home. Where else would I have been at nine at night? I don't think I managed to say one word to him for the entire phone call. At some point one of us hung up and I'm willing to bet it was me, because I remember distinctly having the phone curled in my arms against my stomach as I hunched over on my knees and sobbed into the ground.

The rest of the house was dead silent. I was too afraid of Jens to leave the bathroom. What was I going to do when Viktor got here? I couldn't even imagine. Would Viktor come to me? Would he climb through the window and carry me away like a maiden in distress? Probably not. But still, I had to get out of the bathroom, and ultimately the house, somehow.

So I crawled and crept over to the bathroom door and looked under the crack. I'm not sure what I expected to see, but it was dark. No lights were on in the house. Where was Jens?

I saw the headlights of a car approaching and I knew it had to be Viktor. I recognized the shape of the lights as they shined through the window and reflected off the bathroom mirror, catching a glimpse of my ghastly face in the process. What would Viktor think of me? One step at a time. I couldn't worry about it yet.

But since Viktor was nearly here and Jens's location was a mystery to me, maybe I could make a break for it and be fine.

I cracked open the door. The sound of the latch was the loudest thing I could possibly have ever heard. No movement. Nothing stirred. So, like a cockroach, I skittered toward my front door. And that's when I heard Jens.

"Where the fuck are you off to?"

Though his voice chilled me, and rooted me to the spot, I was *right there*. I was just a threshold away from Viktor. I just had to open the door.

With every ounce of strength that I could possibly muster, I ignored Jens and fumbled with the door handle. It had been locked. I never locked my door. *Jens.*

"I asked you a question, Niði."

There was no way I could have turned around in that instant. I was too frightened to move. I struggled with the door instead. Something as simple as twisting a door handle should have come easy, but my clammy hands slipped against the cool metal. Behind me, I heard the crunch of fabric and scuffle of boots.

I had to get to Viktor. I had to get out. The blood rushing through my ears suffocated all other sounds into distant, muffled drones.

It was so difficult to see. To hear. To breathe.

I have to get out.

Still scrambling, I felt the door handle twist under my fingers. *Viktor.* He really was here. He was opening the door. I had never felt more relieved than in that instant. And as soon as the door swung inward towards me, I stumbled and nearly crashed into Viktor standing in front of the open doorway. He sidestepped and caught me with an arm before I completely fell out onto the stoop.

The stomping behind me stopped. Everything stilled. Outside the thrashing of my heart, silence.

Viktor was here. He would protect me.

I slid away from his arm, though, and struggled not to sprint to his car. The last thing I heard before slamming the door shut at my side was Jens screaming at me. "Whore! Fag! Bitch!"

He threw quite the loaded thesaurus of insults my way. None of it really registered, though.

I stuck my head between my knees and slipped into a world of horrid cries, curled up right there in the car.

I don't know what happened between Jens and Viktor next or how we got back to Viktor's house. Jens wasn't brave enough to take on Viktor; I was an easy target. Viktor was not.

At some point during the drive, I sat up and drooped back against the car seat. He hadn't said a word yet. Neither had I. Both of us just stared out of the windshield in silence. Because his home was on the edge of town, we sat in that silence for a long while.

I vaguely remember him getting out of the car to unlock and push open the gate that led to his property. The rusted thing got stuck. He slipped in the mud and fell on his face. I think I almost laughed. Almost. He swore. I think.

Viktor came back into the car and drove it forward a bit. Got back out. Closed and locked the gate behind him. Got back in the car. Drove up to his front door. Got out. He opened my door for me. I was still in too much shock to get out on my own. He guided me up the steps. Unlocked the front door. Let me in. Locked the door behind him. Took me by the hand and led me to his bedroom. Sat me down on the bed. I think he went to get me a glass of water. That's when I passed out.

When I woke up again, I was under a sheet and a blanket, and some recently applied bandages adorned my face and arms. There was a glass of water next to me on the bedside table. When I sat up, I felt a world of hurt in the pounding of my head and throbbing of all my new bruises and scrapes.

I recalled all the times when I'd seen Viktor's arms covered in bruises as a child. Was this how he always felt? This thought made me mourn for him and start to cry again. Softer though. Silently.

"Are you crying, Niði?" He spoke from a distant corner of the room, startling me from my thoughts, and from the dimness of the lamplight, I saw him sitting on a sofa. He must've showered and changed clothes at some point because his hair was damp and he was in a fresh pair of nightclothes.

I didn't answer him.

He rose from his spot and came to sit at the edge of his bed next to me. He waited for me. As always.

I loved him. I missed him.

Still weeping, I took his hand. How I wished that I never wasted my life with Jens. How I wished I never left Viktor.

I wanted to know everything I'd missed. I wanted to know what happened in those five years. I wanted to know how Viktor felt. About me. About everything. Anything. I think my mind had been cracked open like a coconut and I just needed the closure. Not from him, but from Luna. And Jens. And everything Viktor and I hadn't been able to share with each other. The memories we never got to make. The memories I still wanted to make.

"What happened when we stopped talking?" I asked.

And Viktor told me. He told me everything, from his brother's issues to his father's apologies, and everything in between. He spoke more than I'd ever heard him speak in my entire life.

The gaps began to close and with every story, scraps of aching feelings began to make sense.

"Why didn't you tell me back then about Aleksi and your father?"

I could see that he was uncomfortable, just by the way he was looking around the room. But he answered me once he'd gathered his thoughts. "I didn't know how I felt about any of it back then. I didn't want to tell you until I knew what to say. I never meant to keep anything from you…But I wanted to talk about our future more than I wanted to talk about my brother and his problems. I was being…I wasn't thinking about your feelings. I'm sorry."

"Oh, Vik…" I had to gather myself before responding, something resonating in my heart about the way he'd apologized *to me*. While I was thinking of what to say and wiping fresh tears from my cheeks, I leaned my head against his shoulder. Something about his sturdiness helped me focus a little. "Do you know why I stopped responding to you?"

"No." He shook his head, then said, "Well, I didn't know then. I was just confused and…I was…I felt very sad about it. Luna actually told me she told you to stop talking to me."

"Really?" I asked, "When?"

"Recently. When you saw us from your hiding spot."

I managed a ghost of a laugh at this. And I sensed that Viktor might have smiled.

"It's why we started arguing in the first place, but…Anyway, I understand now. It's alright."

But his acceptance hurt me to hear. I didn't feel like I deserved it, though now I admittedly blamed myself less for what happened. I had made the decision to cut him off, yes. But it wasn't entirely my fault. Viktor didn't think it was, at least. That level of acceptance hurt in its own way. "It's *not* alright. It shouldn't have happened."

Then Viktor started crying, too, and it was the third time I'd ever seen it. He wept just as silently as I did at the moment. We cried together. I don't know for how long, but, I think we both needed to let it out.

When he was done crying, he asked me what happened with *me* in those years. I told him that I'd met Jens, my mother passed, and that was really it. I certainly gave him as many details as he'd given me, but a lot less had happened to me than to him, honestly.

We sat for a moment longer in a comfortable silence again. Hand in hand.

"Hey, Vik?"

"Yeah?"

"…Did you kill Jonas Jonsson?" I had to know. I had to know for sure. Neither of us said anything for a very, *very* long while after that.

But, then, Viktor toppled me over back onto the bed and in an instant he was on top of me with that grin, the very one that I adored. He bowed his head down to kiss me and, since I wanted him to, I let him. He captivated me so thoroughly, despite the darkness of my question and the questionable delight of his response.

But he hadn't answered my question.

So, I asked again, "Did you kill Jonas, Viktor?"

"Do *you* think I did?"

I couldn't look away from his smile as I stared up at him, our faces so close, pinned beneath him. His stupid crooked tooth that I love. His stupid scrunched eyes. I loved him and the sight of him, everything about him. Even…Even if…

I sucked in a deep breath, held it in. I said, "I do. I think you did."

"Would it bother you if I had, dear *Freyja*?"

I wish he hadn't have made my heart pound with that nickname. It was my favorite nickname. Despite the surge of anxiety that came with addressing the confession I meant it when I said, "No."

He released me and collapsed onto the bed next to me with a dull *whump.*

"You know," he said, and I swear I could *hear* the smile on his face as much as I could see it. "During the investigation, they found all that fucking child porn all over his house. Everywhere. Absolutely fucking disgusting… And, he was…He was going to…" The smile faded from his face as he spoke. The words got caught in his mind as he tried to make himself heard.

"I asked Lærke directly if she was afraid of him," Viktor continued, his voice now falling softly along with his waning smile.

I didn't have to ask him to continue. "She…told me she was…"

"Do you…" I didn't want to ask this, but I had to know all the same. "Do you know if he…?"

Viktor rolled to his side to face me directly and put his arm around me. He looked upwards toward the headboard, then left to the ceiling, back ahead, up, left, up, left. It took him a moment to gather himself and I couldn't bear to finish the question.

"…I don't think so…"

"But…"

"Do you think I shouldn't have killed him?"

Now it was my turn to reflect. "I think that you wanted to protect Lærke, and you did just that."

He smiled slightly again, but didn't quite release the slight furrow in his brow. He said, "That's not what I asked."

"You're right," I responded.

"I couldn't let him hurt anyone else. I had to do it."

With a little shuffling, I curled myself closer to Viktor until I was right up against him. I really didn't know what to say, but I sincerely wasn't bothered by his confession. Rather, I couldn't answer whether or not I thought that he should or shouldn't have committed murder. I had realized that it really didn't bother me in the slightest that he had killed someone. It just didn't matter to me. I had been so terrified months ago, but now? I had to say that I agreed with him, that the man probably needed to be killed. In fact, part of me had hoped that he had done it. Was this wrong of me? Probably.

Then again, maybe it wasn't. Jonas wasn't a good person, his death was mourned by few, if anyone even mourned him at all, and he had been a danger to Lærke's wellbeing. To *my* wellbeing. I think, as he always had, Viktor must have acted logically when he killed Jonas. The more I thought about it, the more I admired him for it. Viktor had to protect his daughter and Jonas Jonsson was a ticking time bomb. He did what he had to do.

It had been me that had pointed the finger at Jonas, anyway. I had unleashed my rabid dog on him and now I had to bear some of that responsibility on my shoulders too.

"Viktor?"

He looked right at me. With his smile faded but still present, his stormy eyes still full to the brim with kindness and warmth. How could I have ever been afraid of him? He didn't look like anyone that could cause harm. He didn't look like a killer to me. When I gazed at him, all I saw was the same dark-haired boy I'd always been in love with. My Viktor. My Óðr.

"I love you," I said.

"I love you, too," he responded.

"I know." I know what I had to do. I knew how I felt. How Viktor felt. And I knew for certain that everything had to change. I had to protect myself. I had to protect Viktor and our future together.

Opening his mouth to speak, Viktor looked a little like he might cry again (out of happiness) but I stopped him.

"I can't be with Jens anymore." My mind was made up. Viktor's face hardened as he examined my face, but my conviction only grew stronger. "I have to go home tomorrow. There's something I have to do, but can I stay with you tonight?"

"Yes." His answer was immediate.

"Stay here with me?"

"If that's what you want, it is easily done."

I know this now as I knew it then, there isn't a thing in the world that Viktor wouldn't do if his beloved *Freyja* wished it. It had always been that way, but this was the first time I felt comfortable accepting that. And so, I like to count that as the first night we spent together as an official couple.

But I don't need to tell you what happened.

● At the End of the Dream

The next morning I went home as I said I would. The dawn air was crisp and chilly, as it often was in our cold little town, and the golden sparkle of the sun reflecting off the dewdrops was a more beautiful sight than I could have ever imagined. Viktor drove me back, letting the small, tin-like speakers in his car serenade us with whatever rock CD he had in the car. We didn't need words anymore, and I think both of us were always more comfortable sitting in silence together than we ever were with senseless chatter.

As it was, he dropped me off and gave me a twitched corner of a smile. I kissed him goodbye and went to face my problems head on for the first time in years.

Jens wasn't there at the moment, but I knew he would be eventually. I'd called him, after all. Somewhere in the night prior I made my plans. I suppose you could call it premeditated to an extent. And, as I prepared for Jens's arrival, I didn't feel an ounce of guilt. I was fed up and things had to change. I decided to take a page out of Viktor's book.

Now, as you might imagine, Jens was a little more than pissed off when he came to see me and he reeked of alcohol, as if he'd done nothing but drink and drink and drink up until that point. As predicted. He was weak.

Regardless, I let him continue drinking as he hurled insults and dishware at me. It didn't terrify me like it had the night before and he missed most of his throws, anyway. If anything, Jens's drinking and outbursts, while violent and cruel, mostly now just reminded me of a toddler throwing a tantrum. I wondered if this sense of calm is what Viktor felt before he killed Jonas. Had it come just as easily to him?

Perhaps it was because I knew that as he drank pint after pint, that I so kindly poured for him, I knew that he was drinking of my garden's most lovely plants. That there was enough atropine and solanine in his drinks to knock him down a few times over was satisfaction enough for me.

I knew what had to be done and how to do it.

Would this come up in a toxicology report? Would this come back to haunt me? Perhaps my plans had been a little rash, but he needed to die and I don't think I could overpower him. This was the way I had to do it. I'm sure Viktor would have done it for me, had I asked, but this was something I needed to do myself.

Poison or otherwise, I felt like it wouldn't be too big of a stretch to say that Jens discovered his university sweetheart had been cheating on him, and that that had led him into a depressive binge-drinking spiral. He couldn't handle the sadness and decided to end it all, perhaps by poisoning himself. Wasn't that a beautiful story and a fine way to end things?

After enduring all that he'd done to me, watching him collapse and succumb to the slurry of toxins in his body was more than satisfying. Of course he hadn't died immediately and, admittedly, watching the struggle and foam before he passed out was a little too visceral for my liking, but what can I say? If this is what it took to protect myself and be rid of Jens, then how could I not do it? If Viktor could get away with murder, why couldn't I?

Of course, hours after the deed had been done and Jens lay curled up on my floor like a battered fly, smacked out of the sky to curl up and flop wherever he landed, I called Viktor. I'd been prepared to kill Jens and I'd felt not a hint of remorse, even as he seized and spasmed to the floor. I had to do this. He deserved this. Anyway, I called Viktor.

Yes, I was crying. Yes, he came to me immediately after making up an excuse to Malika (or maybe it was Sindre) as to why he needed a last-second babysitter for Lærke. Yes, he took care of everything else for me. He always did.

After he came to my house, Viktor spent most of the day on the phone, speaking in hushed tones with someone I didn't know. I sat in the living room and tried not to cry.

Eventually, a man I'd never met came to my house to help Viktor deal with Jens. From what I remember, the man had a strange sense of humor and a one-sided banter with my Viktor. They seemed to get along well enough, though.

The man stuffed Jens into his trunk, drove off, and I never saw him again. I'm thankful that he helped Viktor clean up my mess. I'm not sure I could have gotten away with it or not had I just left Jens to rot on my kitchen floor.

Anyway, Viktor took me back to his home after everything was said and done. I think I must have slept for twelve hours once we arrived. All I know is that once I woke up and the dust had settled, Jens wasn't my problem anymore. Jens was gone. Good riddance.

◉ Goodbye

After the whole fiasco with Jens, life mellowed out for me. Outside of tying up a few more loose ends and living cautiously for a while, there were surprisingly few snags in my situation. I'll spare you the details.

Viktor and I made our relationship official and spent a lot of time healing together. There was so much for us to catch up on from all those lost years and there were many 'firsts' that we wanted to share with each other.

So we did just that. Our first date. Our first anniversary as a couple. Our first trip to Iceland together. Lærke joined us for that one. At first, Viktor and I weren't sure how to break the news to her. Sure, she already knew from her father that he and I had been friends since childhood, but I wanted to navigate the jump from 'my dad was childhood friends with my teacher' to 'my dad is dating my teacher' with a little caution. Viktor respected my hesitation and need for tact initially, but he ultimately ended up telling her outright one day.

Lærke asked him if he was going to get married someday, you know, in that precocious way children often ask difficult questions and Viktor, being honest and direct as ever, answered. He said to her that he was going to marry me and that led to another line of excited questions on her end. I gained a tiny wedding planner that day.

It came as a great surprise when she announced at the start of class when I next saw her that Viktor and I were engaged. It wasn't the most orthodox proposal, but I'm glad it happened that way. I'm glad Lærke was involved and I'm glad that she was happy about it.

After that cat shot out of the bag, the three of us spent a lot more time together outside of the classroom. Getting to see Viktor with his daughter truly was a delight and being accepted so readily by her meant a great deal to me, too. I don't mean to brag, but I've always been her favorite teacher, so maybe I shouldn't have worried so much about confessing to her that I was in a relationship with Viktor. A few more years passed before we got married, but thankfully those years remained peaceful and uneventful. The three of us celebrated a lot of holidays and birthdays together, read a lot of books, and shared a lot of quieter memories.

After we got married, we had to decide where to live, you know? Thanks to you, Viktor owned his home, whereas I was only renting my late grandmother's home. Unfortunately, my father wasn't really thrilled to hear that I'd married another man, so he asked me to move out and that sorted out the whole issue. I moved out of my grandmother's home and into Viktor's home as soon as I was able. It was a little sad at first, to leave that house and its beautiful garden behind, but I think I'm much happier where I am now. I have a new garden, one that Lærke helps me tend to, just as I used to help my mother.

Since Viktor and I are married now, though, I thought it might be nice to come talk to you. We never got to meet when you were alive, but for what it's worth, I think you did your best when you were raising Viktor and Aleksi. I've learned a lot about you over the years, and while I can't say I agree with some of your methods and a few of your choices, I think I can understand why you did some of what you did. At least, a little bit. I know that Viktor's forgiven you, so I will try to as well.

I'm sure you want to know how Aleksi's doing as well, but I don't know for sure. I know Viktor has stayed in contact with him, but they don't speak very frequently. The last I heard, Aleksi was working on his rehabilitation and had chosen to stay out of town for a time. I hope he comes to visit you sometime, too, if he hasn't already.

Maybe Viktor will come visit you and tell you his side of the story. He drove me here today, you know? But he's waiting in the car because he still gets a little emotional about your passing.

I know it meant a lot to Viktor when you reached out to him and apologized to him during those college years. I'm sorry that your time together was cut so short. I've never really been able to make amends with my father, and he never really forgave me for being the person I am, so I'm really happy that you and Viktor could at least reconnect for a short while.

Would you have been alright with it if you had known that Viktor was in love with me? Would that have bothered you at all? Maybe it's better if I don't know the answer.

Either way, I know I've been rambling here for quite some time now. Gosh, I think my voice is sore, you know? But, I wanted to have a chance to meet you, even if it's just me talking to thin air like a loon.

I think you would have liked the gravestone that Viktor picked out for you, by the way. It took him years to pay for it and finally have it installed, but I think it was worth the wait. I don't know if you can see it, so I'll just describe it to you real fast.

It's a lovely black granite stone and there's an etching of your boat on it, your name, of course, the dates of your birth and death. Viktor carved his initials into the side of it. Apparently, he did that as soon as the stone was installed, and he hasn't been back since. I think he cried for a whole day after that, so it might still be too difficult for him to come see you like this, but try not to hold it against him.

He's never been great at looking death in the eye, so give him time. That's about all I had to say, really. I just thought that I might share a little bit to you about your son that you might not have known. And, well, since I'm his husband now, I thought you might want to know a little bit about me too. Can you believe it, though? Lærke is about to start secondary school this year. I really hope you get to meet her soon.

Well, goodbye for now. I'll be sure to bring Viktor with me next time. I'm sure he has a lot to tell you.

About the Author

M. Lalli Lassegard is a polyglot with a penchant for collecting linguistic textbooks. Though his linguistic devotion eats most of his time, he spends what remains of it delving into the depths of obscure musical groups from the 80s. He has a song recommendation for any occasion and will not permit anyone to think otherwise. When writing, Lassegard strives towards a minimalist writing style and places specific emphasis on the emotional exploration of characters. He draws inspiration from themes surrounding sociolinguistics, language identity, and social ambiguities. His focus is on the mundane aspects of every day life and how they can be either crushingly oppressive or delightfully surreal. While his work can often delve into grim topics, he tries to weave a sliver of hope into his stories. Above all, he hopes that his writing can resonate with others who may be in need of validation or comfort.

M. Lalli lives somewhere in the North. He spends a lot of time reading, writing, and doing little else. Linguistics is one of his favorite hobbies. On days when the weather is nice, he likes to speak German to his cat.

Find more about M. Lalli at: https://lalli-land.neocities.org/

www.ingramcontent.com/pod-product-compliance
Lightning Source LLC
Chambersburg PA
CBHW011324310726
48973CB00011B/3050